KT-522-509

Staffordshire Library and Information Services
Please return or renew by the last date shown

~~CODS~~ ~~CODSALL~~		

CARIBBEAN
ESCAPE WITH
THE TYCOON

CARIBBEAN ESCAPE WITH THE TYCOON

ROSANNA BATTIGELLI

MILLS & BOON

First published in Great Britain 2020
by Mills & Boon, an imprint of HarperCollins*Publishers*
1 London Bridge Street, London, SE1 9GF

Large Print edition 2020

© 2020 Rosanna Battigelli
ISBN: 978-0-263-08476-4

MIX
Paper from
responsible sources
FSC C007454
www.fsc.org

This book is produced from independently certified
FSC™ paper to ensure responsible forest management. For
more information visit www.harpercollins.co.uk/green.

Printed and bound in Great Britain
by CPI Group (UK) Ltd, Croydon, CR0 4YY

For my beautiful daughter, Sarah,
a strong, shining star.

CHAPTER ONE

"You sit here and don't move, Adrien," Chanelle heard a deep voice say at the table across from hers. She had just been looking out at the coast from the deck of the luxury cruise liner *Aquarius*, a ship she'd never dreamed she'd be a guest on.

"I'll be right back with something yummy for the both of us," the man said with a laugh. "I'll give you a hint: it rhymes with *nice dream...*"

Chanelle looked up, curious to see the face that matched the voice. But she only saw the back of the man's head. And below the golden-brown hair that curled at the ends, a firm neck and muscled shoulders that were distractingly discernible under his turquoise shirt. His perfectly fitting black linen trousers emphasized his strong legs.

Before he turned toward the ice cream machine, a young lady passed by wearing a red bikini and a filmy white cover-up that barely covered anything, and gave the man a big smile. She said something to him, and Adrien's father stopped to talk to her, giving Chanelle a glimpse of his chiseled profile and groomed shadow. And his quirky smile and narrowed eyes.

Chanelle's stomach muscles contracted involuntarily, and her pulse quickened, followed immediately by a feeling of guilt for her physical reaction to a guy who was married and yet flirted with other women.

Despicable. And practically in front of his child...

Her attention was diverted by the *vroom, vroom* sounds of the man's son as he moved his miniature racing car along the table. Adrien was a cute little boy, with bright blue eyes and short, golden brown hair, the same shade as his dad's. At one point, he backed the car up and let it go. The car skidded off to the far end of the table, and the boy immediately jumped on his chair to reach across to get it. Chanelle turned in alarm toward his father, but he was now concentrating on filling two cones, the woman gone.

Chanelle's heart skipped a beat. Adrien was

so close to the ship railing… What if he took a tumble over the edge? Her heart leaped into her throat when she saw him begin to straighten, and without any further hesitation, she closed the distance between them in two strides and clasped his arm.

"You need to come down—"

"What exactly are you doing?"

Chanelle heard the deep voice directly behind her. Only this time it lacked the light, playful tone he had used with his son. Before she could react, the child had wrenched himself away and was scrambling off the chair and running to his father.

Chanelle turned to face them awkwardly, feeling a flush bloom across her cheeks. The man had set down the cones and was embracing Adrien with one arm while staring at Chanelle, his eyebrows furrowed above icy blue eyes. "Why were you grabbing him?"

Because you weren't there, making sure your son didn't end up losing his balance and tipping overboard, Chanelle wanted to retort.

She felt her jaw muscles tensing. "I wasn't grabbing him." She looked at the man steadily, willing herself to sound calm and not defensive. "He had jumped up to get his toy car, and I was worried that he'd lose his balance and fall." She gazed at the boy, whose face was puckering as he looked at his shoes. "Or topple over."

"He was in no danger. I had my eye on him." The man's eyes narrowed, and Chanelle felt as if she were staring at two brilliant blue laser beams.

Your eye was on a red bikini, she wanted to retort. She felt her cheeks fire up as the stormy blue of his eyes intensified.

"I was closer to him than you," she said, trying to keep her voice steady, "and from where I stood, he looked perilously close to the edge." Chanelle bit her lip. "Look, I was just trying to protect him. One wrong move and he could have—"

"I get the point," he said, putting up a hand. His tone lacked its previous gruffness, and his eyes seemed to have softened. "Thank you for your valiant gesture."

Chanelle's eyebrows lifted as she stared at the man who was staring down at her. His eyes were a startling turquoise, matching his golf shirt. Gazing at his bronzed features, perfectly shaped lips and a jawline that reminded her of the sculpted perfection of Michelangelo's *David*, Chanelle felt an inner jolt. A series of jolts. As her gaze slipped downward, she had the crazy thought that with his looks and build, he should be modeling for a living. The top buttons of his shirt were undone, revealing an inverted triangle of golden-brown hair. When her gaze returned to his face, she started at the piercing intensity of his eyes. She looked away, her cheeks feeling like molten lava. He stepped forward and took his son firmly by the hand. The child lowered his gaze again, aware that his actions had caused concern.

"What is going on here?" A thirty-something young woman with bouncy strawberry-blond hair, and clothes and shoes that screamed *designer*, approached them and took Adrien protectively by the hand. She threw a concerned look at her husband.

"Nothing to worry about," he drawled. "I'll take care of it."

Chanelle couldn't help glancing at his left hand. *No ring.* She almost snorted. *No wonder.* He obviously preferred to *look* single… Chanelle's gaze flew to the petite woman.

Did she have any idea that her husband was a playboy?

A rich playboy, from the look of her diamond of at least two carats.

"I'm going to our stateroom. Come on, Adrien," she said brusquely. She lifted an eyebrow imperiously toward her husband. "Vance?"

"I'll join you shortly, Mariah," he said. He released Adrien's hand.

Chanelle stood by awkwardly as the man's wife strode past her stiffly, ignoring her completely. When she and her son had disappeared past the automatic glass doors, Chanelle glanced warily at the man. *Vance.* Nice name. Too bad it didn't match his character.

He had taken a few steps closer, and his brows were furrowed again. Her nose picked up spicy notes of his cologne. A woodsy and exotic fragrance that reminded her of sandalwood and cedar. Chanelle wondered uneasily if, now that his wife and child were not present, he was about to give her a blast for interfering in their business.

Why *hadn't* she minded her own business? The cruise hadn't even begun, and already she was feeling a surge of anxiety. She took a deep breath, bracing herself for a verbal onslaught.

And then his brows unfurrowed. "Have you considered applying for a job on the ship, watching over the children?" he said with a quirk of a smile, blue eyes crinkling at the corners. "I don't believe this cruise line comes equipped with a guardian angel."

Chanelle blinked, distracted by the way the turquoise of his eyes had darkened to lapis and not knowing how or what she should reply. She patted her hair down self-consciously. It had been rather humid in Tampa, and in such conditions, her hair had a tendency to fluff out and get frizzy.

Her emotions at this moment felt just as frizzy, with the unnerving way that he was gazing at her...

"I—I was just trying to prevent a tragedy," she said, unable to keep the defensiveness out of her voice. She straightened, trying to boost her confidence. She was not going to let this—*this womanizer*—try to appease her with his charm. How many other women had he referred to as an angel? "And I'm not sorry I interfered," she added, jutting out her chin.

He stared at her wordlessly for a moment, his eyes narrowing, before shifting his gaze to her engagement ring. His jaw muscles flickered and he seemed lost in thought, and Chanelle had to resist the urge to whip her hand behind her back. Finally he looked up, and pinned her with a curious gaze. "Your fiancé is a helluva lucky guy to have such a caring wife-to-be. He won't have to worry about your future children, with *you* protecting them like a lioness." He gave a husky laugh and then stared at her intensely. "So tell me, since this is a Zodiac cruise, *are you* a Leo?"

Vance watched the extraordinarily long eyelashes of the woman opposite him flutter over green-hazel eyes that sparkled like gemstones. Her glossy lips parted briefly and then shut, drawing his eyes to their perfect dimensions— not too thin and not too wide. And from having observed her stature as he approached—or more specifically, the way she fit into her white jeans and fuchsia T-shirt—it was obvious she either worked out or was just born lucky. He watched as she ran her fingers through her lustrous auburn hair, the movement sending a hint of her perfume drifting toward him, a candy-like scent of raspberry and plum...

She blinked at him as if his question were the last thing she had expected to hear him say.

What the hell was he doing? He didn't really want to know her sign, did he? *No, of course not.*

Vance wished he could take the question back. It was something he might have asked in a more flirtatious situation. And he had no intention of flirting with this lovely but rather overreactive—*and engaged*—passenger. He shifted as a couple strode past them. He should have followed Mariah back to the stateroom immediately. And now he had to think of an appropriate way to end this—

"Sagittarius."

She said it defiantly, her green eyes flashing a silent warning.

He had no choice but to continue this now. "Ah...the Archer," he murmured. "The healer whose intelligence forms a bridge between earth and heaven." He raised an eyebrow. "Let me guess. You're either a nurse or a teacher...or in some kind of caring profession." He stroked his jaw. "Or I'm completely off the mark and you're an astrophysicist," he added with a chuckle.

She wrinkled up her face and rolled her eyes, an attempt—*possibly?*—to conceal her amusement. A tingling sensation spiraled through him. The dimples that had appeared briefly in her cheeks were charming. Whether he liked it or not, she was igniting feelings that he did not want ignited. He forced himself to come back to earth. "Well, are stars your thing, or what?" he said lightly.

Her lips parted, and she had that look of *Why would you even want to know?* She gave him a measured glance. "I don't have time for stargazing," she retorted, "and my job is much more down-to-earth. With no sparkle or glitter."

She hesitated for a moment, and her eyes seemed to darken. He caught the slight crease of her forehead before it disappeared.

"I'm a social worker," she said matter-of-factly. "In child protection." She took a deep breath, and her eyes seemed to blaze in the late-afternoon sunshine. Her mouth opened slightly as if she were about to say something more but then promptly closed again.

Vance surveyed her flushed cheeks. No wonder she had been so quick to act with Adrien. And he had been too quick to jump to the wrong conclusion, asking her why she was grabbing him… "Protectiveness is in the nature of a Sagittarius," he said gruffly, nodding.

She didn't respond, but something flickered in her green eyes before she lowered her gaze.

Vance knew that Adrien hadn't been in danger, but he could understand that from where she had been sitting, it had looked like Adrien was in a very vulnerable position. And she hadn't hesitated in reacting…

Something in Vance's gut told him that if Adrien *had* tumbled over, this vigilant Sagittarian would have plunged right in after him. He had seen that fierce protectiveness in her eyes as she had quickly reached out to stop him. Vance had no doubt that on the job or not, she saw herself as a champion of children, on constant alert to ensure their safety and well-being.

His gaze shifted again to her hands, where she was unconsciously twiddling her ring.

He felt his jaw tensing. "I should let you get back to your—"

Her head jerked up.

"Fiancé."

Her eyes shot green sparks at him before dropping to her left hand. "Thank you," she replied stiffly, her voice sounding far from grateful. She tossed her hair back and turned away.

It was quite the mane, he thought, watching the way the sun made her auburn hair look like copper gold. He had a sudden urge to run his fingers through it. And to talk to her longer, despite the voice in his head urging him not to.

"Hey, there," he called. He waited until she turned around and then flashed her a smile. "I realize I must have sounded harsh initially," he said. "I apologize. I'm protective, too, when it comes to family."

Her eyes widened. For a moment she said nothing and then shook her head dismissively. "No need to apologize. I probably should have minded my own business."

"Well, allow *me* to at least apologize for addressing you as 'Hey, there,'" he said, smiling. "I'm Vance. And I'd like to make it up to you by buying you a drink. What do you say, Miss—?"

She blinked at him wordlessly. When a few seconds had passed and she still had not responded, he frowned. "Is something the matter?" Was he imagining it, or was she giving him a look of disdain?

"I don't have drinks with married men," she said coolly. "And I believe you told your wife you'd join her shortly…"

Vance blinked, momentarily confused, but before he could reply and tell her he wasn't coming on to her, she had turned on her heels and disappeared.

Way to go, Kingston. How obtuse to be offering to buy a guest a drink, given that she was engaged and that she had presumed he was married. From the look on her face, it was obvious that she considered him a creep. Shaking his head, Vance headed inside and pressed the elevator button for the ship's upper level— Deck Thirteen. He glanced at the time on his phone. The cruise director would soon be announcing the emergency assembly drill. All the passengers would be called to make their way to their assigned deck to undergo the required safety routine in the event of an emergency. And soon after that, the ship would set sail.

He had enough time to have a quick talk with Mariah and Adrien and then relax with a glass of wine at the Mercury Bar on Deck Ten. No, he would head to the bar first. Mariah would probably be wondering what was taking him so long, but until she texted, he was just going to take advantage of having some time to himself.

As the elevator opened on Deck Eight, Vance caught a flash of auburn hair among a group of people walking down the hall. He felt his pulse jack up. And then another flash of fuchsia above snug-fitting white jeans. It *was* her. He smiled apologetically when he realized that several elderly women were waiting for him to move to the back of the elevator so they could enter.

Moments later, Vance leaned back in a lounging chair in the Mercury Bar, savoring one of the ship's premium wines. It would kick off his week-long holiday after an intense nine months taking over Zodiac Cruises, his parents' company. Even though he had initially balked when his mother had mentioned plans for a special cruise to formally hand over the reins of the company to him, Vance was looking forward to finally having some time to unwind.

Nine months ago, the life Vance had known

and enjoyed had shattered. His father had had a heart attack after a family dinner. Before he had taken his last breaths, he had managed to tell his family that he loved them.

Vance swallowed hard. The man who had spent so much time away from home—and had relinquished parenting to build his business—had looked at him with piercing clarity for a few moments and rasped, "I'm sorry, son. For everything I said or didn't say to you. For not being there for you as you were growing up. I... I wanted to build the company for my family. Now I leave it in your hands... Will you take it on, son?"

Vance had felt a sharp twinge in his own chest at his father's words, and he had instinctively realized that he needed to forgive his father. The wall he had constructed around his heart over the years, brick by brick, had to give. But something had lodged in Vance's throat, preventing him from expressing any feelings, and when his father passed seconds later, Vance was flooded by guilt that he had not given his father the satisfaction of knowing that he had forgiven him—or at least that he would try to forgive him—and that he would carry on with the company.

That was what his dad had always wanted, to have him working alongside him, learning the ropes and eventually taking over when he decided to retire. But Vance had balked from the beginning, always feeling a disconnect with the man who had barely been around in his youth.

And how could the concrete barrier around his heart even begin to give after decades of reinforcement? His father's quickly uttered words to him as he approached the end of his life were too little and too late.

Getting involved in the company had been the furthest thing from Vance's mind. In high school, when his father had urged him—on one of his rare home visits—to do his community service hours at Zodiac Cruises' headquarters, Vance had declined, preferring to volunteer at a nearby art gallery. His time there had reinforced his interest in the art world, and the sketches he had shown his father to prove his intentions to pursue art at university had met with barely concealed scorn.

"You've got to be joking." His father's sharp laugh as he had tossed Vance's scrapbook aside dismissively had struck him as if he had lunged a fist into his chest. Vance still remembered how he had wobbled backward a couple of steps, slack-jawed and speechless.

"Are you telling me you'd rather be a starving artist?" His father's eyes, resembling gray storm clouds, had bored into Vance. "Don't be a fool." And then he had abruptly left, telling his wife that he had lost his appetite and wasn't going to stay for dinner.

Vance winced at the memory. His father had been harsh with him, but Vance had refused to buckle and eventually graduated with a master of fine arts degree, receiving the highest honors and a substantial monetary prize from the department. His mother had been at his graduation ceremony, and the look of pride in her glistening eyes had moved him, but her effusive words of praise and congratulations could not make up for the fact that his father had not bothered to show up.

Within a few months, a prestigious art gallery in Toronto's historic Distillery District had hired Vance as assistant curator, and his work there, along with his travels, had kept him quite occupied, with very little time to visit his mother save for the occasional Sunday dinner.

The dinner that had proven to be his father's last had turned out to be the same as previous occasions—the atmosphere tinged with tension, stilted conversation and a formality that was never present when he was alone with his mother. Seeing his father—whom he had always categorized as tough and uncompromising—reduced to such a vulnerable and conciliatory state had been a shock. His father's deathbed request had immobilized him, and Vance had barely had time to process the request before his father passed.

Vance took a gulp of wine. He had never wanted to get involved in the family business, but the irony was that after the funeral, Vance had spent every waking moment trying to prove himself worthy of following in his father's footsteps. For his mother's sake, he had tried to convince himself repeatedly. He was doing it for her, to keep the business running as smoothly as possible. And maybe to assuage the guilt that had surfaced knowing he hadn't given his father the satisfaction of a positive response to his last request as he had taken his last breaths.

And to do the job properly, it meant that he had had to temporarily give up the lifestyle he had previously enjoyed, which his father had not approved of. And his job at the art gallery.

It had been too late to make a vow to his father, but not too late for Vance to carry out his promise to himself.

So for the last nine months, Vance had worked twelve-hour days at headquarters in Toronto and had undertaken several cruises, mentored by every department head of Zodiac Cruises. He had been surprised at how much he had enjoyed learning the workings of the business, and he had started to think of ways that he could put his art and history background to good use in the company...

His mother had planned *this* cruise to officially acknowledge Vance in his new position. "Your father wanted this, remember?" she had reminded him several times when he had claimed that he didn't have time. "His dream was to pass the reins as president of Zodiac Cruises over to you himself one day..."

Vance felt a fresh stab of grief and the familiar swirl of guilt in his gut. What had he really known about his father's dreams? His feelings toward his father were so convoluted. He was sure that he had felt every possible emotion when it came to his dad: bitterness, disappointment, abandonment, even hate in his adolescent years. He had never understood the man…a man who had chosen work over family.

What's done is done, he told himself. He had another drink of his wine and willed the memory of his father's last moments to vanish. As soon as that image had dissipated, green-hazel eyes flashed in Vance's memory. Why did his thoughts keep returning to *her*? For nine months, he had stayed clear of women, focused entirely on the company. He hadn't agreed to take a break and go on this cruise with the notion of resuming his past lifestyle…

And yet he had impulsively told her he'd like to buy her a drink. What the hell had he been thinking? And he had completely ignored the clear fact that she was engaged. Vance scowled. It was obvious that his playboy habits hadn't been completely extinguished…

He couldn't help wondering what her fiancé was like. Did he run his fingers through that blaze of hair? Did it get wild and tangled when they—?

Taking a deep breath, Vance forced the image out of his mind. He should have never agreed to this cruise. It was frivolous, considering the projects that needed his attention back at Zodiac headquarters...

Vance rolled his neck to one side and then the other. Maybe after the emergency drill, he'd relax in his private whirlpool. He felt tense around his shoulders, and the warm jets would be a welcome relief... A bit later on, he'd either order room service for dinner or they could dine at one of the specialty restaurants if Mariah preferred.

And then they would proceed to the Milky Way Theater, where the ship's troupe of dancers and singers would be performing a medley of songs from the '60s to the '80s. Classic hits from iconic singers. It was a great first-night show, and he would be giving a brief welcome to the audience before it started.

And maybe the Sagittarian might not be there to distract him...

CHAPTER TWO

CHANELLE STOOD BY the railing on Deck Eleven, her gaze shifting from the lapping waters of the bay to the magenta-and-gold sunset as the Tampa Bay skyline receded in the distance. She had decided against joining the cruise director and other staff and the probable swarm of guests at the Sail Away party on Deck Twelve after the emergency drill. She wasn't in the mood to mingle just yet...

Chanelle closed her eyes, letting the repetitive sound of the waves soothe her. Her thoughts were interrupted by a soft giggle in a far-off corner. Two darkened forms exchanged a kiss and wandered off hand in hand. She sighed. Could she not have picked a holiday where she wouldn't be reminded at every turn of her failed relationship?

She bit her lip. Much as she had wanted to blame Parker for not being sensitive enough to her work commitments, she had had to face the truth: that she had invested more time and energy in her job and not enough with him.

"I've met somebody at the gym…" He had dropped the bombshell seven months ago. And he'd told her he would be back the next day to get his things. Everything but the engagement ring he had given her.

If all had worked out with Parker, she might have been planning her wedding now, or even enjoying her honeymoon…instead of cruising alone, Chanelle mused, taking a deep breath.

But it hadn't worked out, and she had to admit—if she were to be totally honest—that she was relieved.

Not that she had felt that way at first.

Hurt and feeling betrayed, she had wanted to analyze what had gone wrong with their relationship and had checked out the self-help section of a local bookstore. One title had immediately caught her eye, as Parker had often accused her of being overly sensitive. And soon after delving into the book, Chanelle had discovered that she had many of the traits that the book identified…some that she had been aware of and some—she had realized in wonder—that she had exhibited even in childhood.

She'd also learned things she hadn't known: that highly sensitive people had nervous systems that were more easily activated by sensory stimuli. Which had explained why certain smells were unbearable, or why intense sunlight or loud music or people could be so jarring...and why her skin couldn't tolerate certain fabrics. No lace or wool for her! Or most synthetic materials. All this had illuminated her as to why she'd ended up with a skin rash or migraine at times...

Chanelle had learned that highly sensitive people—or HSPs—processed their experiences and feelings with greater depth and emotional intensity.

Given such sensitivities—not only physical, but emotional also—was it any wonder that her line of work had pushed her coping mechanisms to the max? And that Parker hadn't been able to cope? The book had outlined how challenging it could be for others to understand and empathize with an HSP. It was challenging enough for an HSP to deal with their sensitivities, and relationships could present even greater testing grounds...

Her relationship with Parker hadn't passed

the test. Neither one of them had been solely to blame, though. She had been too focused on her work—there was no denying that—but Parker could have at least been honest with her and broken things off *before* getting involved with someone else. That would have been the *decent* thing to do.

And it had been this last thought that had finally convinced Chanelle that Parker hadn't been the right man for her. After the initial shock and sting of betrayal, Chanelle had accepted the fact that Parker was not the guy she was meant to have a happy-ever-after with.

He had betrayed her trust. She deserved better.

This realization had come before the acknowledgment that she had burned out on her job. And her parents, who were on the other side of the globe on an extended trip to visit relatives in Australia, hadn't been there to comfort her for either her breakup with Parker or her lingering emotional distress after a traumatic case involving two siblings and their neglectful parents. Meredith, Chanelle's employer, had kindly advised her to consider a leave even months before this particular case, having observed the classic signs of burnout becoming more prevalent in Chanelle. But Chanelle had insisted she was fine, telling herself that she needed her work more than ever after Parker had left...

She had been wrong, of course. She should have heeded Meredith's advice from the beginning. Chanelle sighed. After consulting with her doctor, Chanelle had taken a leave, "to be assessed on a regular basis." This was not a sign of weakness, her doctor had asserted gently, but a step toward ensuring her emotional well-being. Having a job that dealt with the trauma of others required particular diligence in maintaining physical and emotional health and balance in one's own life.

Enough! Chanelle was tired of thinking of the circumstances that had brought her here. And she needed to keep Parker out of her thoughts. She didn't want him on this cruise with her. She was over him.

She had tucked the engagement ring he had left her in her purse months ago and had slipped it on her finger momentarily, wondering what she was going to do with it. And then, before she could put it back in her purse, she had become distracted by the incident with the child and his distracted father.

Perhaps what she really hadn't gotten over was the fact that another man had dumped her. The first one had been her biological father. Her mother had revealed the story to her when she had felt Chanelle was ready. His name was Trevor, and upon hearing that his girlfriend Katie—Chanelle's mother—was pregnant, he had promptly broken up with her, claiming the baby wasn't his. He had accepted a job out of town right after college graduation and never returned, leaving Katie heartbroken. Fortunately, Chanelle's grandparents hadn't abandoned Katie, and Chanelle had grown up missing a father in her formative years, but living with a set of grandparents who cherished her.

She had just turned twelve when her mother married a furniture dealer called Martin, and although Chanelle had initially been reluctant to trust him—there had been a couple of men Katie had dated before him who had caused Chanelle some anxiety—Martin's easy and joking manner and obvious devotion to her mother eventually won her over. Chanelle's faith in men had been temporarily restored, but now she had to admit to herself that Parker's decision to break up had stirred up a flurry of latent feelings that could be associated with her father's rejection of her. Her social work and psychology studies had not been for nothing, she thought, her mood darkening as she watched the swirling waters from the deck.

Two men had abandoned her. One, her father, who hadn't even wanted to acknowledge that he'd had anything to do with her conception. Who had chosen to run away from his responsibilities to her and her mother. And Parker, who had left her for another woman. Both had run away from the promise of what was to come—the birth of a baby and the birth of a marriage, respectively. Neither the baby nor the marriage had been given a chance...

Chanelle's work had helped take her mind off the latter. She had pushed herself to the limit, convincing herself that the children she was protecting, or rescuing from a parent or parents who were unfit, depended on her. And she had no intention of abandoning them.

She had tried to be a superwoman, she realized, and had driven herself into a state of burnout. And she was having a hard time coming to terms with not being able to do her job.

Who am I? She shook her head and gripped the deck railing. Her job had been everything to her. *What do I do now?*

Chanelle squeezed her eyes tightly at the prickly sensation behind her lids but wasn't able to stop a few tears from slipping down her cheeks.

"Hey, there…"

Chanelle didn't need to make the quarter turn to see who the approaching footsteps belonged to.

The distracted father/playboy.

"I can't have anyone on my ship looking so sad." He stopped a couple of feet away from her.

Had she heard correctly? *My ship?* No, it couldn't be…

Chanelle quickly wiped her eyes. How embarrassing that he had seen her in such a state. She looked beyond him, expecting to see his wife.

"Has something happened on board to upset you?"

Why did he care? And what could she possibly tell him?

"I—I'm okay," she managed, her voice wavering.

His eyes swooped down on her and narrowed. "No, you're not."

She stared at him, startled by his directness. Something thudded in her chest. "It's not something I feel comfortable discussing with—"

"A total stranger?" He raised an eyebrow. "Look, you don't need to discuss anything with me. But now that I'm here, I'd like to set the record straight." He took a step closer. "I wasn't trying to come on to you earlier...and seeing someone in tears on a cruise concerns me."

Chanelle looked beyond him again, the butterflies in her stomach rising in a swirl. What would his wife think if she suddenly showed up? She took a step back. "I appreciate your concern, but you don't need to worry about me." Actually, she *didn't* appreciate his concern, but the words had left her mouth before she could stop them.

"The expression on your face worried me." He rested an arm on the railing and glanced at the water before meeting her gaze again. "It was more than sad—it was almost a look of desperation."

Chanelle's eyes widened as his words hit her. *Hard.* "You thought I was going to…" She glanced at the black depths of the bay. She had been momentarily sad, yes, but desperate, no. *No.*

"I would have stopped you," he said huskily. "Or dived in after you, new suit and all."

"You wouldn't have had to." She held up her chin defiantly, trying to prevent herself from gazing at him from the neck down.

His piercing blue eyes had a hawklike intensity, as if he were trying to determine if she was lying. "Good to know." His brow smoothed out. And then his eyes narrowed again. "I don't mean to pry, but if there is a problem between you and your…" He glanced at her ring finger.

It suddenly hit her. He had noticed her engagement ring during their first encounter…

His words struck a nerve. Chanelle bristled. Was this…this Romeo…actually implying that she was having issues with her fiancé? What business did he have to butt into her life? She felt an inner heat surge through her veins and upward into her cheeks.

"Look, I hate to be blunt, but I don't appreciate you trying to find out if there is a problem in my relationship. It's really none of your business." She felt her cheeks tingle. Usually the precursor to their becoming flaming red. "And if you don't mean to pry, then don't."

"*Touché.* I apologize, Miss...or Ms...."

She threw him an incredulous glance. Did he not realize that she didn't want to keep talking to him? He just raised his eyebrows and looked as unruffled as she was ruffled. It didn't help that a portion of her brain was registering how good-looking he was in his charcoal-gray suit and salmon-colored shirt and black tie. She heard herself sigh in frustration.

"Chanelle." There! Now maybe he'd go away and leave her alone.

He opened his mouth to respond but closed it when his cell phone buzzed. He retrieved it from his pocket to glance at it. He messaged back and then looked at Chanelle again. She moved away from the railing, and he did the same. Surely he didn't intend to follow her? She was planning to head over to the Ristorante Mezza Luna for dinner, having made reservations at this specialty restaurant when she had booked her cruise, deciding that she deserved to pamper herself.

And after this double encounter with this playboy, Chanelle was anxious to start relaxing. She nodded dismissively and walked toward the glass doors, deciding to freshen up in her stateroom before heading to the restaurant. She saw his reflection and felt her stomach muscles tighten. Inside, the lights of the chandeliers made her blink.

She headed to the elevator, and when she turned, her heart jolted. Vance was striding toward her, but his phone buzzed again and he slowed down to glance at it. Chanelle hurried into the elevator, but before the door closed, she saw him glance up and across at her, his eyes glittering like the chandelier crystals above his head.

Mariah had texted Vance the first time to say that she was almost ready. He had laughed inwardly. His sister's sense of time was faulty at best. "Almost ready" could mean "I need another half hour." But she had surprised him with her second text that she was in the restaurant and had already ordered them drinks.

Vance had messaged her that he needed a few extra minutes.

He glanced at the closed elevator doors before striding over to a recliner near a lounging nook and thought about what had just happened with Chanelle.

Chanelle... What a soft, feminine name. A name fit for an angel, except that there had been nothing angelic about the look she had flung at him.

Why had she appeared so dejected when he had first spotted her? His heart had begun to thump against his rib cage when he had seen her gripping the railing in that isolated corner of the deck... And at the sight of the tears glistening on her cheeks, the thump had turned into a hammer. He had been ready to leap toward her, and then she had turned to look at him...

Relief had swirled through him like an electric current. He had wanted to wrap his arms around her—an irrational impulse, considering he didn't know her, but he couldn't deny that he had felt a surge of protectiveness that had stunned him.

He had immediately noticed that she wasn't

wearing her ring, which was why he had presumed that she and her fiancé had had some
kind of disagreement, or maybe even a fight.
No wonder she was sad, especially if she was
having problems in her relationship. Had she
ended the engagement? Had *he*? Vance's jaw
tensed at the thought that Chanelle's ex-fiancé
might have cheated on her. Maybe that was
why she seemed so irritated with *him*. Maybe
she was projecting her anger and hurt on him
or any other male who crossed her path or even
looked at her the wrong way…

But why was this Chanelle taking up so much
space in his thoughts? He squeezed his eyes
shut for a moment, then relaxed them. Tensed
his shoulders, then let go. He did this a few
times, and after a few deep breaths, he opened
his eyes.

Vance checked the time and sprang to his
feet. He had kept Mariah waiting far too long.
At the entrance of the Ristorante Mezza Luna,
the maître d' greeted him and led him to a
far table, where Mariah was already enjoying
a glass of white wine and a plate of cheeses
and spiced olives. "Sorry I'm late, sis," he said
with a rueful smile. He sat down, and after the

waiter had filled his glass, he explained what had happened earlier with Chanelle, reassuring Mariah that Adrien had never been in danger. "How is the little munchkin?"

"Adrien's having room service with Mom, then they're going to watch a movie and go to bed early," Mariah said.

Vance nodded and took a drink of his wine.

"Don't look now, Vance!" Mariah lowered her voice to a whisper. "There's the lady who couldn't mind her own business."

Vance set down his wineglass and tried to ignore the skip of his heart beat. "Mariah, I told you, she was just worried—"

"Okay, okay. I can't fault her for that, *Sir Vancelot*." She chuckled as he rolled his eyes at her childhood nickname for him.

Vance turned casually. Chanelle hadn't spotted him. She was smiling brightly at the maître d' and nodding. She had changed from casual wear to a long magenta skirt with a shimmer of sequins along its flaring hem and a body-hugging black top that accentuated her slender neck and feminine curves. The maître d' led her directly toward the table next to his and Mariah's.

Mariah's phone rang, and Vance could hear that it was his mother's voice on the other end.

Chanelle suddenly stopped walking. Vance met her incredulous gaze. He held up his glass and nodded with a polite smile. It was obvious from the rosy hue of her cheeks that she was flustered to be seated so close to *him*. And Mariah.

Chanelle gave a brief nod and looked away, focusing on what the maître d' was telling her about the wine selections. She murmured her choice, and he nodded. "Certainly, Miss Robinson."

Vance didn't know if it was the wine or the discovery of Chanelle's last name that ignited a shiver of heat inside him. He said it under his breath. Chanelle Robinson. He liked the way it sounded. Soft. Silky. Just like that mane of hair tumbling over her shoulders.

The next time his glance coincided with Chanelle's, he flashed a smile and nodded. Her eyes fluttered briefly, and she responded with a nod that made him think of a robin giving a tentative peck at the grass. Her cheeks were now almost as red as a robin's breast, and the way her arms lifted and then dropped helplessly made it clear to him that if she could fly away, she would.

"Mom says Adrien feels a little warm. Probably too much excitement today," she murmured, arching her eyebrows in Chanelle's direction. "I'm going to check on him. If he's okay, I'll meet you in the theater."

Vance stood up and met Chanelle's eyes. Even in the dimmed lighting of the restaurant, they were stunning, their green-hazel depths looking like a mystical pool from an enchanted land.

"I hope you're enjoying Mezza Luna's fine offerings, Miss—Chanelle," he said as they approached her table. He gave her a casual smile. "Oh, and please allow me to introduce you. Chanelle Robinson, this is Mariah Kingston... my sister."

CHAPTER THREE

CHANELLE STRUGGLED TO keep her surprise in check. *His sister?* And how did he know her last name? Oh, yes, the maître d' had said it...

Feeling awkward at the realization that she was just blinking back at him, Chanelle turned and offered a tentative smile to his sister.

Mariah held out her elegantly manicured hand. "Nice to meet you. *Again.*" She blew her brother a kiss. "I'm going to go and check on Mom and Adrien and then head to the Milky Way Theater. See you in a bit, *Sir Vancelot.*"

Chanelle watched her leave, a petite swirl of pink silk and ivory linen above shapely legs and stiletto heels that Chanelle wouldn't hazard to wear. When she had walked into the restaurant and had caught sight of Mariah sitting across from Vance, something in Chanelle's chest had deflated, and she had considered making an excuse to the maître d' and filing out of the restaurant. The last thing Chanelle had counted on was bumping into the both of them so soon after the earlier incident...

Discovering that the lady he was with was his sister and not his wife had caused a thumping against her rib cage that almost made her look down at her chest self-consciously.

Vance put his hand on the chair opposite her. "May I?" he said, his blue eyes appearing more like indigo in the muted light of the restaurant.

"Um..." She glanced from him to the waiter. "Okay," she replied slowly, irritated both by his question and by the way her pulse had spiked.

How could she tell him, with the waiter standing right there, that she had been looking forward to a quiet dinner?

Despite feeling flustered, Chanelle couldn't help thinking how drop-dead gorgeous he looked in his gray suit with the salmon-colored shirt making a striking contrast with the extraordinary purple-blue of his eyes. They reminded her of the rich hue of the delphiniums in her summer garden.

"Will you be joining Miss Robinson for a glass of white wine, sir?" the waiter asked Vance, naming the vintage she had selected.

Vance nodded his approval. "I could tell you were a woman of good taste," he said, flashing Chanelle a smile. "May I join you?"

Chanelle hesitated before giving a curt nod.

Vance turned his gaze back to the waiter. "Put it on my tab, Luciano."

Chanelle gazed from one to the other and opened her mouth to protest, but Vance put up his hand firmly. "That wasn't necessary, Mr.... Vance," she said when the waiter had left.

"No it wasn't, Miss *Chanelle*." He leaned forward. "It's just my way of thanking you for looking out for Adrien."

Chanelle frowned. "You weren't too pleased about me getting involved earlier."

He clasped his hands under his chin and gazed at her squarely. "I admit I may have overreacted." His eyes glinted. "I'm sorry. Can you find it in your heart to forgive me?"

Chanelle was at a loss for words. From the slightly amused tone of his voice, she didn't know whether he was being genuine or mocking her. And at the same time, she was trying to process the fact that he wasn't married after all, that Adrien was his nephew, and that his earlier offer of buying her a drink wasn't the act of an unfaithful womanizer.

Which meant that she had overreacted as well.

So maybe you should apologize, too, her inner voice suggested. *And if this hunk wants to treat you, let him! You have a choice—you can tell him to take a flying leap, or let him spend his money on you... Live a little! And if he flirts with you, give it back to him. You've forgotten how to have fun, girl!*

As she framed some words of apology in her mind, the waiter reappeared with the wine. Vance tasted and approved a sample and nodded for the waiter to fill their two glasses. He held his glass up and waited for Chanelle to clink hers with his, but she ignored his cue and went ahead and took a sip.

"Mmm…" Chanelle closed her eyes momentarily, unable to control a little shiver. She was entering into unknown waters, she warned herself. She felt her nerve endings tingle and realized she could either take this opportunity to enjoy the cruise, or leave it…

The excitement stirring in her stomach gave her the answer. She wasn't going to mope around anymore. She was going to loosen up a little. She had always been too serious growing up and had proceeded with caution in every aspect of her life, even when she had left home. Chanelle breathed in deeply, her chest expanding, and she felt like a Sagittarian warrior, ready to rise up to anything or anyone. Especially one like the Dionysus sitting across from her, twirling his wineglass with a gleam in his bewitching blue eyes.

Vance looked at Chanelle as the waiter asked her if she had decided on her entrée. She chose a seafood risotto, and Vance decided to order the same for himself. "Excellent choice, Chanelle. It's one of my favorites," he said after the waiter had left. Chanelle paused, her eyes widening as if she had just realized that he was not going to be leaving after he finished his wine. And the slight flutter of those long lashes made him wonder how she was feeling about that...

"This is even better than the wine I had in my room." Chanelle's words came out in a rush. "And I thought that one was superb. I must say I'm impressed with the perks on this cruise.

The complimentary gift basket was such a lovely surprise, with the scrumptious chocolates and all those other goodies." She flashed him a smile before taking another generous sip of wine, her eyes a combination of amber and emerald as they blinked at him above the rim of her glass.

Vance certainly hadn't expected this...this about-face. But then maybe Chanelle was trying to drown her sorrows, the sorrows of a broken relationship...

"Cheers, *Sir Vancelot*," she said with a tinkling laugh as she raised her glass and cocked her head at him, her hair cascading down like a shimmering curtain. His heart did a flip, and he had to stop himself from extending his hand to let her rest her head against it.

Vance gazed at Chanelle's flushed cheeks and long eyelashes. He had no illusions that they were fluttering for *his* benefit, yet he couldn't help being mesmerized by their languorous movements, allowing him glimpses of the heady hazel depths of her eyes.

He coughed, and feigned a frown. "Now don't *you* go calling me by that silly name, Chanelle. My sister likes to torment me occasionally with it, with maybe just a *little* less frequency than when we were kids and playing with my medieval castle." His eyes narrowed. "I'm neither a sir nor a chivalrous knight."

Chanelle gave him a shy smile that made his stomach muscles contract. "You were ready to rescue me earlier... That proves you're chivalrous." She averted her gaze to help herself to an olive and immediately exclaimed at its spiciness. She ran her tongue over her lips and fanned them with her hand.

As Vance watched her mouth, a spiral of heat flicked throughout his body. The waiter set down their plates, and after thanking him, Chanelle gave a self-conscious shrug and dug into her risotto. Vance suppressed a smile. It was refreshing to see a woman enjoy food, unlike a couple of the willowy high-fashion models he had dated who had pretended to be happy with a few pieces of lettuce and a couple of carrot sticks.

"Are you a pescatarian?" he wondered aloud.

"No. I just stay away from red meat."

"So no bacon for you."

"I'm into *baking*, not bacon." She laughed, lifting her wineglass to her lips.

He grinned. "Since you've ventured into the world of puns, perhaps you should consider a job in comedy..."

The humor suddenly disappeared from Chanelle's face. Her eyelids fluttered briefly, and she stared down at her plate. He saw her jaw muscles flexing. When she looked back up, her eyes were glistening.

Vance set down his glass. "I'm sorry, Chanelle. Did I say something wrong?"

She put her fork down. "No, I'm... I'm..." She shook her head. "I'm just a little down about my job." She cocked her head at him as if she were trying to ascertain whether she could trust him to tell him more.

"It's a tough job," he said gently. "Dealing with vulnerable children and harsh situations day in and day out. I can only imagine—"

"I thought I would last longer than this..."

"You left?"

"I'm on a leave. Burnout." She sighed. "I love kids, I love seeing bad situations turn out for the better, but it hasn't always worked out that way...and it has affected me off the job as well."

"You're only human." He controlled his impulse to reach out and tap her reassuringly on her arm. "It's obvious you care, and with your background, it's no wonder you were alarmed when you saw Adrien on that chair. Your devotion to children is admirable," he added softly.

"I'm too devoted, according to my fiancé." She bit her lower lip and leaned back. "I mean my ex-fiancé. He broke off our engagement."

"I'm sorry to hear that," he murmured. "You've been through a lot."

"I have to take some of the responsibility," she said, her mouth twisting. "I spent too much time working."

And her fiancé hadn't liked it.

Vance watched as Chanelle slumped forward, her chin resting in one hand. Her earlier levity was gone, and he suspected the wine might have had something to do with her shift in emotions. He couldn't imagine her spilling all this personal stuff to him otherwise.

He glanced at his watch and sprang out of his seat. "I'm sorry to cut this short, Chanelle, but I have to be somewhere else. Five minutes ago, actually," he added ruefully. "I'll let you enjoy your dessert in peace. By the way, will you be catching the opening night's performance in the Milky Way Theater?"

"I—I...maybe," she said cautiously before picking up her fork again to dig into her risotto.

"Okay then," he said slowly, nodding. "Maybe I'll see you there. *Arrivederci.*"

Vance glanced at her left hand. He was about to add something and then decided against it. Feeling a strange tug in his stomach muscles, he rose and left.

Vance sprinted toward the theater. He had been totally absorbed—*distracted*—with Chanelle Robinson. Thank goodness he had looked at his watch or he would have been inexcusably late, missing his cue to address the guests on this special cruise.

In five minutes, the cruise director would be welcoming the crowd, then he'd be introducing him, and Vance would share the reason he and his family were on board the *Aquarius*. They had decided to keep it from the media and had simply wanted to have a relatively small celebration of Vance's official position as president. They had decided on a five-day cruise just to relax, mingle with their invited guests—who had promised to keep the event under wraps—and have a gala evening mid-week, when Vance's mother would announce her retirement and formally pass over the business to Vance.

The uninvited guests were in for a surprise, for the gala would be open to them also, in appreciation for their patronage and, for some, their loyalty in returning to Zodiac Cruises for a holiday. In fact, what seemed to be trending was for Zodiac faithfuls to book a different Zodiac ship each time they cruised. Vance had already met a group of nine forty-something women who had already cruised on four of the ships in the fleet. They had been friends since high school, and although they didn't all live in the same town, they reunited every year for their one-week cruise.

Vance had smiled at them earlier in the lobby of the art gallery. As he had strolled by, he had heard one of them whisper, "He doesn't have a ring. He must be unattached…" And one of her friends had chortled. "Lucky gal who gets to attach themselves to *that*. I'll be having sweet dreams tonight…and of course, *I'll* be the lucky gal." And at the resounding laughter, he had stifled a chuckle and had gone to chat with the art rep.

Now, entering the slightly dimmed theater, Vance looked around. Spotting Mariah, he made his way to the third row in the orchestra section. Mariah smiled at him and continued checking her messages on her cell phone. Vance sat back and thought about what the ladies had said.

"He must be unattached."

Well, they were right. For the most part. At the moment he was not seeing anyone. His last relationship had fizzled out after his father had died. Brianna was a wealthy socialite his mother had invited over one night, someone she had thought might be a good match for Vance. They had seen each other for several months, but Vance hadn't been ready for a serious commitment, and Brianna *had*.

If she had been the right one, wouldn't he have wanted to settle down?

His mother had hinted more than once—and not too subtly—that perhaps he should start trying to find someone who could become more permanent in his life. He was thirty-four, after all, and didn't he get tired of dating one beautiful woman after another? Vance smirked at the memory of the comment she had made once—that he changed women as often as he changed cars.

"You're not getting any younger, son, and neither am I. I don't expect to have grandchildren when I'm too old to be able to lift them. Or play with them."

Occasionally she had taken a sterner approach, pinning him with her steel-blue eyes.

"You can't be a playboy all your life, Vance. It's time to get serious...serious about settling down."

Vance had instinctively known that his mother had felt responsible for indulging him and his sister in all ways. They had grown up spoiled and entitled, he had heard her complain to his father, and now they expected that lifestyle to continue.

Especially Vance. At least Mariah had married and blessed her with a grandson. She could be high-maintenance at times, but being a parent had tamed her somewhat. Now Vance, on the other hand...

A week after his mother had voiced her concerns, his father had died. And the lifestyle

Vance had known had come abruptly to a halt. There were matters to take care of, both personal and business, and his mother had been too distraught to deal with any of them. It had been left to Vance to make the funeral arrangements and to be the strong shoulder for both his mother and sister.

Brianna had expressed sympathy, but she was used to a certain pace in her life, and she had expected Vance to keep up with her high-profile social events and private parties a few weeks after the funeral.

But the passing of his father had taken the desire for partying right out of Vance. The immensity of his father's responsibilities and the esteem in which his business associates had held him had made Vance acutely aware that *his* involvement in the company had been peripheral at best. And when it had been time for the last goodbyes, and his mother, sister, brother-in-law and nephew had walked away, Vance had stayed behind to quietly reiterate the vow he had failed to make to his father before he died.

Soon after, when he had told Brianna about his intentions and that he couldn't make a firm commitment, Brianna had skipped out of his life.

Vance checked the time on his phone. One minute before the show... He glanced at Mariah and saw that she was texting her husband, who hadn't been able to join them on the cruise, as he was tending to business in Europe.

Vance glanced around and was pleased to see that the theater was filling quickly. His eyes narrowed as he searched the moving groups for a sign of Chanelle. And then he checked himself.

Why did he even care if she attended the opening or not?

The orchestra started up, and a minute later, cruise director Jake Ross walked out on stage. At his cue, Vance strode to the side door that led to the stage and waited for Jake's intro. Jake warmed up the audience with his jokes and stories about funny experiences onboard, and when the laughter had subsided, his tone became more serious.

"Ladies and gentlemen, I have the distinct pleasure of welcoming you to the *Aquarius* and to our opening night show here in the beautiful Milky Way Theater. You are in for a few surprises this week, starting with the man you are going to meet shortly. He is someone who has taken on the monumental task of leadership of Zodiac Cruises these past nine months since the passing of Mr. Bruce Kingston—Zodiac's founder and president—proving with his unreserved determination, razor-sharp focus and relentless efforts and inexhaustible energy that he has everything it takes not only to continue in his father's fine footsteps, but to leap beyond. He will reveal his vision for the company during this cruise, and I am sure that you will be as excited as the staff of the *Aquarius* and of the entire fleet of Zodiac Cruise ships to hear about his initiatives and to celebrate during this special cruise." He turned toward his right and extended a hand. "And now, please join me in welcoming Mr. Vance Kingston, acting president and co-owner of Zodiac Cruises!"

Vance stepped out to a resounding applause. He was moved by Jake's words and the crowd's enthusiasm, and after thanking them for their presence and participation in a Zodiac cruise, he explained why he was there, and what they would be in for.

At the loud cheers of approval and whistles,

he gave a bow, and when he raised his head, his gaze landed on a guest who was just sitting down on the far end of a middle row in the right-hand section of the theater.

Chanelle...

Had she arrived in time to hear him from the beginning? He pulled his gaze away from her. Ordinarily, he had no problem addressing a large crowd, but somehow, knowing she was there, he suddenly felt awkward. He hadn't told her anything about himself, and he couldn't help wondering if she'd be feeling awkward as well when she realized who he was.

He finished up his address and thanked the audience again. His gaze swept casually over the crowd, and for a few seconds, Chanelle seemed to be looking straight at him. As the orchestra started up with a musical number that would take the audience through decades of Broadway theater productions, Vance strode off the stage, the cue for the *Aquarius* dancers to appear.

He and Mariah had chosen seats near the front on the left-hand section of the theater. Vance was too far away from where Chanelle was sitting to even get a glimpse of her. As he sat down, he exchanged smiles with Mariah, who squeezed his arm in approval. The chandeliers were dimmed, and the dancers burst onto the stage in a swirl of sequins, lights and music. Vance sat back in the plush seat to take in the spectacular opening, but as the dancers spun past, it was a pair of hazel-green eyes that danced before him…

CHAPTER FOUR

CHANELLE HAD ALMOST made up her mind to call it an early night after her dinner and go back to her stateroom. She knew that she had indulged in more wine than usual, and she had been aware that her responses to Vance had been less careful as a result. It made her cringe to think of how she had giggled and made a ridiculous remark about him being chivalrous. And how she had called him Sir Vancelot. And if that wasn't bad enough, she had nattered on about her job and her past.

By the time she had finished the restaurant's signature tiramisu, Chanelle had felt like she could easily go straight to bed. Her appetite had been quelled in the most decadent way, and the rich food and the wine had made her quite mellow. The restaurant had almost filled to capacity and the alternating levels of voices had started to become overwhelming.

She had been wondering whether she could

handle sitting for over an hour in the Milky Way Theater when her eyes had started to droop. It had been an emotional day in more ways than one, and she had debated whether she could even take the sensory stimulation of the opening night performance when all she wanted to do was lie on her bed with the balcony door open and listen to the relaxing sound of the waves...

But Vance Kingston will be there, remember?

Chanelle had smiled and thanked the waiter. As she had walked out, the image of Vance's inky-blue eyes as he had said earlier, "Maybe I'll see you there," had made her stop in her tracks. It might have been a totally casual statement, but the thought of encountering Vance again had made her heartbeat quicken, even if he'd be there with his sister.

Why was he on this cruise with his family? Was it a special birthday for his mother? Chanelle had wondered if she'd get the chance to find out more about Vance on the cruise.

She had kept walking, her steps suddenly lighter, her drowsiness gone. Outside the restaurant, she had checked the time. The show had started at nine, and she had already missed ten minutes. But a glance toward the theater doors had confirmed that people were still filing in. She had heard laughter from the audience, and the thought had occurred to her that it might do her a world of good to laugh, especially after spending the last few months dealing with the reality of job burnout and, a couple of months before that, her broken engagement with Parker.

Chanelle's counselor had encouraged her to find opportunities to lighten up her life with events that would bring her joy and laughter. She needed to balance her life, have more fun…

At the next peal of laughter, Chanelle had ignored the voice in her head that told her it had been a long day and she should just go to bed. She had followed a family into the theater and spotted an empty aisle seat to her right.

Settling in her seat, she had caught the last few minutes of the cruise director's comedy routine before he began his announcement. She had started at the mention of Mr. Bruce Kingston, and a few moments later, felt a greater jolt at hearing the name of Vance Kingston, "acting president and co-owner of Zodiac Cruises."

Her gaze had riveted to the man walking across the stage.

Her Vance?

What a ridiculous thought. He was not *her* Vance. But he *was* co-owner of the cruise line. She had felt a flutter in her chest as she recalled his earlier words: *"I can't have anyone on my ship looking so sad..."* So she *had* heard correctly.

Chanelle had joined the rest of the audience in clapping their welcome, and when the noise had subsided, she could hear the thumping of her heart against her ribs. Even from a distance, the way he had looked in his tailored suit had caused her to draw in her breath, and her cheeks had flamed at the tingling that had begun navigating throughout her nerve pathways.

Three women in the row ahead of her had nudged each other and exchanged whispers about the "hunky owner" of the cruise line. Chanelle had difficulty trying to listen to Vance while overhearing descriptions about his sexy attributes.

She had been relieved when they had stopped their chatter and focused on what Vance was saying, allowing her to focus as well. She had listened to his deep voice welcoming the crowd, thanking them for having selected Zodiac Cruises for the very first time or for their loyalty in returning.

He had proceeded to give a summary of his father's vision and accomplishments, and then his voice had wavered for a moment when he declared that his focus was to keep his father's company thriving. As the audience responded with enthusiastic applause, Vance had scanned the theater with an intensity that made Chanelle's insides flip. Could he be searching for *her* in the crowd? she had mused. He *had* said, "Maybe I'll see you there…"

She had shaken her head at her silly presumption. Vance Kingston was for all intents and purposes *president* of the cruise line. He had obviously just been showing her the courtesy he would have displayed to anyone else on the ship. But after her embarrassing behavior in the restaurant, she'd vowed to make every effort to avoid him.

And then she had frozen. For a moment, it had looked like Vance was staring right at her, and the applause and people around her had became muted as she held her breath at the possibility... And then he had shifted his gaze and continued speaking. He had promised the audience that they were in for some special perks and surprises on this particular cruise, and that the cruise director would keep them informed every day of what was happening, along with the daily bulletin they would be receiving.

Finally, Vance had thanked them again, told them to enjoy the opening show and, flashing the crowd a smile that elicited a couple of whistles, had walked off the stage.

Vance was nowhere to be seen as the crowd exited the theater, and Chanelle had to admit to herself that despite her vow to avoid him, she felt a little disappointed. She returned to her stateroom and had a quick shower, her earlier drowsiness completely gone. While her hair was drying, she searched online to see what she could find out about Vance Kingston. Chanelle discovered that he had been a person of interest in the world of the elite for quite a while, frequenting exotic locales and attending high-profile events—dealing with art, cars and entertainment—that attracted the rich and famous, many of them women.

Some of the headlines had proclaimed him to be one of Canada's most eligible bachelors, not only ruggedly handsome, but easygoing and extravagant, indulging in a variety of interests and activities all over the country. One week he'd be seen skiing in Whistler, British Columbia, among Hollywood celebrities, and the next he'd be at some posh literary or art event in Toronto or at Montreal's jazz festival. From the look of any one of the women in his company, it was obvious that they were happy to share the spotlight with him.

After checking more recent sites, Chanelle learned that Vance Kingston had been employed as head of acquisitions at an art gallery in Toronto's Distillery District until the death of his father nine months earlier. Recent articles described him as almost reclusive now, totally focused on carrying on the family business.

Chanelle turned off her cell phone and ventured out on the balcony. She stared down at the water, swirling and cresting and catching the light of the moon in shiny arcs and squiggles. She could have stayed there longer, but her common sense reminded her that a good night's rest had been what her doctor and counselor had recommended.

Lying under the bedsheets with her balcony door partially open, Chanelle listened to the slurping water sounds and thought about the opening night show by the *Aquarius* singers and dancers. It had been spectacular and as dazzling as a top-rated Vegas show. But the image that kept returning to her mind was that of Vance Kingston. The way he had sounded, his voice velvet smooth. And the way he had looked, tall and male-model gorgeous, his golden-brown hair glinting under the spotlight. Flashing that killer smile at the audience that had made her stomach flip and scanning the crowd with brilliant blue eyes that she knew could change like the waves.

Seeing Vance up on that stage had been the first shock, and learning that he was soon to be the official president of Zodiac Cruises had been the second. The memory of him in that tailored suit and the sensual thrum of his voice as he had addressed the audience ignited a tingle throughout her body.

Although it was a balmy night, Chanelle shivered and pulled up the covers. She nestled into a side position, sinking into the comfortable pillow with a sigh. There *had* been a lot of pulsating lights and energetic musical numbers, but she had left the theater less affected by the overstimulation than she had expected. *And more affected by Vance Kingston.*

Chanelle had hoped for a relaxing holiday where she could shake off some of the built-up stress of the past and try to come up with a plan for the future. She *had to* make a decision where work was concerned. She couldn't remain on a leave indefinitely. Getting away on a cruise had seemed like the perfect opportunity to resolve the issue of whether to return as a front-line child protection worker or to seek work in an area that wouldn't consume so much of her time and energy.

But how relaxing could this cruise be, knowing that she might cross paths at any time with Vance Kingston? Would he be dining at the same restaurant? Swimming in one of the pools? Catching the nightly shows? And what about the gala? Surely he must have a special somebody in his life who would be here to celebrate his new position with him and his family?

So what? an inner voice interrupted her thoughts. *Why wouldn't you be able to relax? Just because he treated you to some wine doesn't mean he's going to seek you out again.*

And why would he? With his family onboard, and probably a group of close friends and associates, he would hardly be intending to pursue *her*. For conversation or otherwise.

Chanelle felt her eyelids getting heavy. She wondered what it would be like to be pursued by Vance Kingston. And then she immediately chastised herself for having such a harebrained thought. She had other things to deal with now instead of indulging in a ridiculous fantasy about the president of Zodiac Cruises.

She was not interested in anybody pursuing her.

Not. Interested.

The last thing she wanted was to be embroiled in a relationship.

Chanelle exhaled noisily. What a ridiculous notion she had had earlier, that of encouraging herself to flirt with Vance Kingston. The wine had been to blame for that. It had addled her brain, loosened her tongue, and of all the people who could have witnessed her temporary lapse of sanity, it had to have been the *president* of Zodiac Cruises.

She closed her eyes and scrunched them tight before releasing the tension, willing the image of cobalt-blue eyes to disappear from her mind.

Vance tossed his jacket onto his couch and loosened his tie. He ran his fingers through his hair. He was happy with the success of the opening night show, but he would have been even happier if, after the show, he had been able to speak with—

He stopped himself. What was he thinking? Just because he had spent some time with Chanelle Robinson before the show didn't mean that he needed to connect with her afterwards. He gave a curt laugh and shook his head before heading to the shower. He had other things to think about, like the upcoming gala.

Mariah had brought up the subject as he was walking her to her stateroom after the show. She had glanced at him speculatively and said she was surprised that he hadn't invited "anyone special" to accompany him on the cruise.

"Currently, there are no contenders in that position," he had replied wryly, raising an eyebrow. "Taking over for Dad has been my priority... And even if I wanted to, there's no time."

"Mom said that Brianna phoned the house the other day. She said she hadn't been able to reach you on your cell."

"I don't have time for Brianna," he had replied dismissively. "Or her universe." He had had no problem inhabiting her universe in the past, but somehow, he had no inclination to get caught up in it again.

In the shower, Vance let the streams of water relax his shoulder and back muscles. Thoughts of Brianna dissipated as frames of Chanelle flicked through his mind like a slideshow: Chanelle reaching for Adrien, her brow creased in alarm; the way she had cocked her head and smiled at him when she called him Sir Vancelot; the flicker of genuine concern in her eyes when she talked about her line of work; the look of her walking into the restaurant with that curve-hugging black top and magenta skirt that matched the color of her lips exactly; and—

He groaned. Chanelle was a witch, she had

to be, to have put some kind of spell over him that had her appearing in front of his eyes even when she wasn't there. *Damn!* He had vowed that he wouldn't let women distract him from what he needed to accomplish at Zodiac Cruises... There was too much at stake, especially his self-respect. He had made a promise to himself, and he had every intention of keeping it.

And for the past nine months, he had succeeded. After Brianna, there had been no one. Oh, he had been all too aware that there were women who still had hopes when it came to winning his favor, but he had not succumbed to their discreet and not-so-discreet invitations.

Despite the fact that he had sometimes felt tempted...

He knew it was guilt over his lack of involvement in the business before his father had passed away that had something to do with it. *Everything* to do with it. And his failure to make a deathbed promise to his father to take over the business. Yes, guilt had put a giant wedge between him and any thoughts of involvement with another woman.

Vance stepped out of the shower, briskly

towel dried his hair and wrapped the towel around his hips. He sauntered over to his minibar and extracted a bottle of ice wine. He poured himself a small glass and walked out to his balcony.

Was Chanelle out on hers? Or sleeping?

An image of her lying on the bed with her lustrous hair spread across the pillow sent a shiver through him. Vance finished the wine and went back inside.

He replaced the towel with a robe and stretched out on his bed, his hands cradling the back of his neck. There was something that made Chanelle Robinson different from the women he had dated in the past.

She's not into herself, he realized with a start. She was *real.* No artifice or pretensions. No glossy manicure or designer clothes. Not that there was anything wrong with a glossy manicure or designer clothes. In his experience, it was the *attitude* that sometimes accompanied them that was pretentious.

And Vance hadn't detected any of that kind of attitude from Chanelle. She seemed down-to-earth, and it was obvious she had been dedicated to her job. He frowned as he pictured her walking into a home and having to remove the children because of neglect or worse. Having to deal with belligerent parents...

Vance breathed in sharply. Had Chanelle ever been in danger? A spiral of anger shot through his veins, quickly followed by that surge of protectiveness again. With a groan, he vaulted off the bed. There was no use even attempting to turn off his thoughts and go to sleep. He glanced at the clock. Not quite eleven o'clock.

He considered running around the track on the upper deck and then changed his mind. He tried reading a book, but his mind kept wandering. Frustrated, he put the book down, flung off his robe and slid between the cool sheets of his bed. With a deep sigh, he allowed thoughts of Chanelle to slip in beside him...

CHAPTER FIVE

WHEN CHANELLE WOKE UP, her eyes followed the light to the balcony. This was their first at-sea day, and all that was visible were water, clouds and sky. The clouds were low and tinged pink and coral. So pretty... The sun was just rising, a hazy golden orb veiled by the shifting clouds. Chanelle slid open the door wider and stepped onto the balcony. She stood by the railing, breathing the fresh air and watching the clouds' transformations.

She went back inside and changed into a mint-green swimsuit, deciding to do a few laps in the pool before breakfast. Now that she couldn't use work as an excuse not to exercise, she could invest some time in the physical fitness department. And she rather relished the thought of having the pool to herself. She didn't imagine too many people would be there this early, including...

Chanelle felt her cheeks prickling with heat

at the thought of Vance Kingston doing laps in the pool alongside her, his muscular arms and chest—

Stop! She frowned at herself in the mirror. "You, Chanelle Robinson—" she pointed an accusing finger "—are pathetic, daydreaming about the president of Zodiac Cruises. Pathetic and ridiculous."

She stuck her tongue out at herself and, after tying her hair up in a ponytail, put on a peach-colored cover-up. Grabbing her beach bag and towel, Chanelle headed to the pool on Deck Twelve.

The view at this height was enchanting, and for a moment, she stood at the railing, absorbed in the gentle collision of pink and saffron clouds as they floated across the horizon. She could do this all day, she mused. *This* was relaxation. And she had had too little of it for ages.

The pool water was balmy, and Chanelle floated for a while, eyes closed, concentrating on the delicious feeling of weightlessness. She would definitely have to make this an early-morning ritual.

Breaking into a front stroke, she swam the

length of the pool and back six times. After rinsing off, she briskly dried herself with the oversized towel and stretched out on her chaise lounge. She would read for a bit, and then she'd go and shower and dress before heading to the Galaxy Café for breakfast.

Chanelle felt her eyelids getting heavier as she was reading. Despite the comfort of her king-size bed, she'd had a fitful sleep, waking two or three times during the night. Turning the book over onto her lap, she let herself drift off, lulled by the water gushing out of the nearby fountain—an Aquarius water bearer...

Vance had always enjoyed working out in the gym first thing in the morning. Besides keeping him fit, it helped him work out his feelings. Whatever frustrations he had had about his father, by the time he had bench-pressed two hundred pounds or sweated through countless repetitions of weight-lifting exercises, his pent-up emotions had been released, if not completely resolved.

His father had been a workaholic. He had spent his energy on building his company, and he had made a fortune with twelve ships in

the fleet, each one carrying the name of a zodiac sign. Zodiac ships were not the largest
of cruise ships, but they had the reputation of
being among the most luxurious. The first ship
to sail had been this one, the *Aquarius*, named
after Vance's sign.

Immersed in the growth of his company, his
dad had left the rearing of his children to his
wife, who had joined him in running the company only after the kids were in school. Vance
had grown up missing a father at school concerts, basketball games and tournaments, and
sometimes at family holidays and special occasions. Like his birthday. And graduation.

Vance had vowed that he would never become like him. His disdain had manifested
in teenage rebellion whenever his father had
shown up, and he and his father had clashed
incessantly. The more his dad had gotten on
his case, the more Vance had acted in outra-
geous ways.

Like buying himself a Harley when he was
eighteen and literally zooming off into the sunset with a motorcycle gang. Not a nefarious
gang, just a bunch of wild and moderately re-
bellious guys like him. They had raced their

way west across the Trans-Canada Highway, enjoying the commotion they caused entering every quiet little town or bar. They had especially liked the attention of groups of women in these locales.

They had happened to end up in Alberta just in time for the Calgary Stampede. They had arrived at the beginning of the annual ten-day festival in July and had enthusiastically joined the cowboy and Western-themed party that attracted over a million visitors every year. They had bought themselves cowboy hats and had whooped it up at the rodeos, parades, concerts and chuck wagon competitions. They had taken their fill of pancake breakfasts, barbecues and gorgeous cowgirls in sexy hats, formfitting jeans and pointy leather boots.

Vance had returned to Toronto with two souvenirs, his cowboy hat and an Aquarius tattoo on his upper back. His father had been none too pleased. He had accused Vance of being a spoiled, ungrateful son, worrying his mother half to death and wasting *his* hard-earned money instead of doing something useful, like working his way up in the company.

He *had been* spoiled. Had spent money without much thought. He had taken luxury for granted, having never known anything but fine food, designer clothes, flashy cars and no shortage of women who appreciated such finery.

Though his adventures with motorcycles had eventually waned, Vance had still wanted to travel. Over the last ten years, he had grown accustomed to visiting exotic locations on a whim and acquiring real estate in Canada—an artist's retreat on Salt Spring Island off the West Coast and a spectacular saltbox house in Newfoundland's Conception Bay. His other home away from home was Coral Haven, the island in the Caribbean that his parents had purchased and where they had built a luxurious villa. The island was uninhabited except for the people employed to travel back and forth from Grand Cayman to keep the villa maintained and prepared for the family's visits.

He was looking forward to spending time at Coral Haven during this cruise. While guests enjoyed the excursion to Grand Cayman, he and his family would spend the day at their villa.

After his strenuous workout, Vance was

ready for a refreshing dip in the pool, located on the same deck. As the invigoratingly cool water splashed over his heated face and body in the pre-pool shower, he glimpsed a figure on one of the chaise lounges.

He squinted and diverted his head from the spray of water. He could see the woman better now: her long, curvy legs, a book overturned on her right thigh, her silky mint-green swimsuit with a flounce ruffle top, wet from her recent swim. Her eyes were obscured by ridiculously large sunglasses, but the ribbons of auburn hair flanking the curves of her face gave her identity away.

Vance felt a drumming in his chest. The *Aquarius* was not a small ship, yet it seemed that at every turn, he was practically bumping into Chanelle Robinson. Vance strode to the deep end and dived into the pool. When he surfaced, he shook his head and glanced toward Chanelle, but she hadn't budged. He began his laps and tried to concentrate on his strokes, but every time he approached the end of the pool near the spot where Chanelle was, his heartbeat seemed to accelerate.

When Vance hauled himself out of the

pool, he was surprised to see Chanelle was still sleeping. Her oversized sunglasses had slipped crookedly down her nose, and her shifting had caused her book to tumble over the chaise lounge onto the floor. He toweled himself quickly and sauntered over to pick up the book with the intention of placing it on the corner of her chaise, when he noticed her stateroom key card at the foot of her chaise. He couldn't help glancing at the number on it.

Chanelle gave a sudden vigorous stretch, catching him soundly on his backside with the back of her hand. He swiveled and met the startled and blinking green eyes that he was beginning to know so well...

CHAPTER SIX

CHANELLE STARED. WHAT was Vance Kingston doing, standing there wearing nothing but his swim trunks and holding her book in his hand? And standing so close that she had whacked him in the rear? Had he been watching her as she slept?

She was mortified, irritated and embarrassed all at once. The last thing—or person—she had expected to see was *him*. Like *this*. Her eyes swept upward past his trim waist, muscled chest and arms and broad shoulders. And disturbingly amused turquoise eyes.

She straightened in her chaise and pulled off her sunglasses. "Excuse me?" she said pointedly.

"Shouldn't that be a statement instead of a question?" he said with a crooked half smile.

Chanelle gaped at him.

"I mean, I don't know if it was intentional, but your backhand was quite forceful. I'm afraid there might be some bruising…" He patted his backside gingerly and made a grimace.

"It was *not* intentional," she said defensively. "Your rear just happened to be in the way."

She frowned. "Why *were* you in the way?" She stared at the book he still held in his hands. "I can't imagine it was because you wanted to borrow my book."

Vance glanced at the cover of the paperback, and Chanelle wished she hadn't brought attention to it. It featured a blue-eyed frontiersman clasping a brown-eyed heroine with windswept hair by her scarlet-corseted waist. Chanelle felt currents of heat sizzling through her, making her cheeks feel as fiery as the dress on the cover.

"I hadn't intended to." He checked out the back cover and then gazed back at her. "I saw it had fallen, and I was just about to carry out my one good deed of the day and pick it up." Vance's eyes seemed to twinkle at her. "But maybe you can lend it to me once you're finished." He handed it to her. "*If* you think I'll enjoy it."

Chanelle took it and placed it on her chaise. He was teasing her, of course. Or mocking her.

She doubted that he was the type to read historical romances. In any case, she was at a loss as to how to answer him.

And at a disadvantage, with him practically standing over her. Chanelle wished she had put on her cover-up. Despite the fact that her swimsuit was a one-piece, she still felt rather exposed, and the tingly sensations within her were causing her to shiver uncontrollably, making her even more self-conscious. She quickly crossed her arms in front of her.

Chanelle heard approaching voices and looked past Vance's shoulder. A family of five was making its way toward the pool attendant. Vance followed her glance. "Time for me to go." He grinned. "Enjoy your book." He turned and strode toward the entrance leading to the elevator foyer. Chanelle's gaze leaped to his broad back, where a tattoo in various blues was splayed on his upper right side. A stylistic double wave design with a realistic-looking splash of water curving below. The same astrological sign as the ship. *Aquarius.* Unable to divert her gaze, she watched the movement of his arm and back muscles until Vance disappeared around a corner.

Chanelle blinked and swallowed and realized she hadn't answered him.

After her shower, Chanelle changed into a pair of navy capri pants and a sleeveless red-and-white-striped top and sat on the balcony to check her phone messages while her hair dried. Her mother had messaged.

Enjoy, relax and pamper yourself, my darling girl. No one deserves it more than you! Love you!

And her stepdad.

Be well, Chanelle my belle, and contact me day or night if you need to, okay, sweetheart? By the way, I'm bringing back a cuddly friend for you... Love you lots!

And he had attached a photo of himself holding a plush koala bear.

Chanelle smiled and then almost immediately felt a wave of sadness engulf her. It was moments like these when she missed her family terribly and felt so alone... As she stared out at the brightening sky, she felt the prickle at the back of her eyes intensify, and a moment later, tears began to trickle down her cheeks.

She *was* alone. Alone with her fears for the future.

Would she be able to return to her job? The work conditions wouldn't change; *she'd* have to change, or she'd end up in the same boat. Chanelle groaned at the unintentional pun, wiped her eyes and strode to the door. *Stop feeling sorry for yourself*, her inner voice chided. *Get out there and start enjoying this cruise!* Chanelle took a deep breath, tossed her hair back and decided to do just that, starting off with a lovely breakfast in the Galaxy Café.

She opened her door and let out a startled cry at the man standing directly in front of her, his hand raised in the knocking position.

Chanelle blinked at the same rate as her heartbeat. She willed her eyelids to slow down, but her heart continued racing of its own accord.

Vance Kingston brought his hand down. He lifted his other one and Chanelle recognized what he was holding—her sunglasses. Her gaze flew to his, riveted by piercing eyes that looked more blue-green now, with the teal shirt he had changed into.

"You left these behind," he said drily, "and I convinced myself it wouldn't hurt to carry out a second good deed of the day. I noticed them when I went back to get my towel and gym bag." He chuckled. "I guess forgetfulness is a trait shared by Aquarians and Sagittarians."

Vance gazed into green-hazel eyes that had a luminescence that hadn't been there earlier. She'd been crying...and her cheeks and nose were slightly flushed. He felt the muscles in his stomach tightening. Could it have something to do with her ex-fiancé?

"How did you find out my stateroom number?" Chanelle's eyes bored into his as she took the sunglasses from him.

"Your key card was on your chaise. I couldn't help seeing the number." Something in her expression gave him a jolt. "Good heavens, I hope you don't think my intentions are dishonorable, Chanelle. That would be most unpresidential of me, don't you think?" He waited for her to reply, but she just continued to stare at him.

"Look, I'm sorry if I caused you even momentary worry," he said huskily, raising his right arm to the doorjamb. "I'm not trying to stalk you, Chanelle. I just wanted to get your sunglasses back to you…and now I just want to make sure you're okay."

The way Chanelle was studying his face reminded him of a teacher trying to ascertain if her student was lying. He tried not to make his mouth twitch in amusement and was relieved when her features relaxed slightly.

She cleared her throat. "Okay. *Fine.* I mean, I'm okay and I—I accept your apology." A corner of her mouth lifted briefly. "I'm sorry if I seemed a little testy…"

"Seemed?" he said, raising his eyebrows.

Her eyes widened, as if she didn't know how to take his remark. "Okay, I'm sorry if I *was* a little testy," she said wryly.

"A little?"

She looked at him incredulously. "You make it seem as if I was biting your head off…"

He burst out laughing. "Interesting choice of words." Something flipped inside him when she laughed back, making her eyes take on an emerald hue. "Speaking of biting…would you care to have a bite with me? Breakfast, that is?"

Her eyebrows went up, as if that were the last thing she'd expected to hear from him. She blinked at him as if he had just asked her a complicated algebraic question and she didn't have a clue as to where to start with the answer. "I—I was just about to go to the Galaxy Café," she finally replied.

"I see," he murmured. He looked past her. "I hope you're finding your stateroom to your satisfaction?"

"It's very nice—roomier than I thought it would be." She nodded and shifted awkwardly in the doorway. "Uh… I forgot my sunscreen in the washroom. I plan to enjoy the sunshine after breakfast, but unless I want to end up with a million freckles, I really should—"

"Would you like me to wait here, Chanelle?" He didn't know what had possessed him to invite her for breakfast, but he had, and there was no way of taking it back.

She hesitated, then shrugged. "You can step inside. I'll just be a minute." She turned and suddenly paused. He followed her gaze to the king-size bed, still unmade, her skimpy teddy tossed on top of the sheets. When his gaze returned to her, her cheeks had already reddened.

He pretended not to notice and immediately sat down on the couch and picked up a magazine. He started leafing through the pages, but out of the corner of his eye, he saw Chanelle walking over and pulling the covers casually over the bed to conceal her teddy. Without glancing his way, she headed to the washroom and closed the door. He heard the water flowing and imagined her splashing cool water over those peachy cheeks.

He was feeling rather heated himself, thinking of Chanelle in that teddy... He tossed the magazine back on the coffee table and leaned back to survey the room. She had some of her toiletries organized neatly on one night table, and there was no sign of her suitcase. He spotted her swimsuit draped over a chair on the balcony and wondered what her reaction would have been if he had been in time to join her in the pool.

The washroom door opened, and Chanelle came out, her hair now held back by a wide navy headband. The casual style emphasized her heart-shaped face and exquisite cheekbones. She had also applied a lustrous red lipstick, and in that snug red-and-white T-shirt and navy capris, she looked like a classic beauty from a bygone era. Innocent and sensual at the same time. Like it or not, that combination sent flickers of desire through him. And the fact that she was unconscious of the effect she had on him made his pulse spike even higher.

She grabbed her tote bag and then suddenly hesitated. "Will you be joining your family?"

He couldn't help chuckling. "Mariah won't be up for a while. And neither will Adrien. As for my mother, she will have already ordered room service at the crack of dawn and is now probably consulting with some of the staff about the gala preparations."

Chanelle nodded, her shoulders relaxing. "I guess we'd better get going, then."

He glanced at the time on his sports watch. "I know the Galaxy Café can get quite busy, especially around this time. How would you feel about trying a spot that's quieter? The Constellation Club, for example."

Her eyebrows shot up. "I… I read that that was for exclusive Zodiac Club members," she said, her cheeks flushing. "I could only afford the basic cruise plan." She gave an embarrassed half smile.

"I can guarantee you won't be turned away," he said solemnly. "If you don't mind going as my guest."

Chanelle blinked. "But…" She looked down at her outfit. "Is there a dress code?"

"Yes," he said with a chuckle. "You have to wear clothes. What you're wearing is absolutely fine, Chanelle. It's not what you think. People aren't parading in black-tie attire and ball gowns." His mouth twitched. "In fact, they're not parading at all. At least not for breakfast."

"I—I don't know. I've budgeted for dining in one specialty restaurant, but this is—"

"On me," he said firmly. "And if you really object, you can offer to do your dishes afterward."

She looked at him hesitantly, then gave a nod, a mix of relief and disbelief in her expression, and Vance felt a warm rush infuse his chest. What he was more accustomed to was seeing a look of smug expectation on a date's face. Not that Chanelle was exactly a date, but it was refreshing for him to know that a lady wasn't expecting him to pick up her tab.

Vance followed her out of her stateroom, breathing in her perfume—a sweet berry scent—and as they walked side by side in the hallway on their way to the elevator lobby, he greeted the housekeeping staff they encountered with a friendly smile and a few words to thank them for the exceptional job they were doing.

The elevator was empty. As the doors closed, he lifted his hand to press the number to the top deck, and as he did so, it brushed against Chanelle's. Their eyes met, and for an instant, he had this crazy desire to lean down and kiss those fabulous lips. When her mouth opened slightly, it was all he could do to force himself to pull his gaze away from hers and press the button.

Finally, after what seemed like an eternity, the door opened, and he indicated to Chanelle to precede him. Her eyebrows lifted, but she accompanied him down the hall without saying anything. When they came to a door marked Constellation Club, Vance pulled his card out of his pocket and tapped it against the brass plate to the left of the door handle. He opened the door wide and smiled. "Welcome to the club, Chanelle."

CHAPTER SEVEN

CHANELLE GASPED IN AWE, her eyes widening as she entered. She couldn't have imagined anything like the room she had just stepped into. The entire ceiling was a glass dome from which were suspended thousands of stars. Chanelle felt like she was taking in a crystal wonderland.

A waiter in a crisp white shirt, black trousers and aquamarine cummerbund greeted them and led them to an oval glass table with silver legs. The upholstered chairs were ivory damask, and as Chanelle sank into one, she gave Vance an incredulous look. "This place is out of this world," she said, expelling a deep breath. Her gaze returned to the ceiling. "There must be a thousand stars up there."

"Two thousand, five hundred, to be exact," Vance said. "Each glass star is crafted by hand in Murano, Italy. They sparkle with the natural light of the sun in the day, and the dome has a fiber optic star ceiling. But on starry,

starry nights—" he flashed a smile at her "—the dome halves retract and the club members are treated to a night under the real stars. And if they're really lucky, they get to see a meteor shower or a shooting star."

"Stunning," Chanelle breathed. She looked around at the gleaming glass tables, each decorated with a multifaceted crystal vase holding a couple of stargazer lilies. In the center of the room, a life-sized and slowly rotating Aquarius statue poured water into a pool from a gilded urn, its gentle gurgling sound adding to the relaxing ambience. The sides of the pool were transparent, and dozens of exotic fish of all colors flitted past each other. Chanelle was mesmerized by their flecks of gold and turquoise, crimson and black, emerald and orange. And their varied shapes and sizes. She could have stood there for hours, enchanted by this giant aquarium. And all around it, the marble floor resembled the ocean, with its varying hues of blue. Sea and sky, she thought. What a heavenly place...

When her gaze returned to Vance, she didn't know what to make of the indulgent look on his face. Was that a flicker of compassion in his eyes? She stiffened. Maybe he was just feeling sorry for her with her limited budget. Perhaps he made it a point to be charitable to a guest every time he went on one of his cruises... She felt a sudden hot prickle inching up her neck.

What had she gotten herself into? She was way out of her league. A few female guests had turned to scrutinize her from head to foot, and from their raised eyebrows and whispered comments to their partners, Chanelle had begun to feel self-conscious. For a moment, she considered making an excuse to leave, but then her inner Sagittarian warrior voice reminded her of her vow to enjoy the cruise and new experiences.

She straightened in her seat and tossed her hair back. Vance was still looking at her with a bemused expression. She picked up her menu and, while scanning it, wished she knew exactly what he was thinking.

She thought she had sensed something more elemental in the elevator, but it must have been her imagination...

The way he was looking at her now was exactly how he had looked at the housekeeping employees. No hint of flirtation in those aqua depths. Yet Chanelle couldn't help feeling con-flicted. She hadn't booked this cruise hoping to hook up with some guy to make her boo-boos better. In fact, after Parker had left, she had vowed to focus on work even more and not bother with men at all. And she had certainly succeeded. Except that the consequence of her increased devotion to her job had taken its toll physically and emotionally. No wonder it was called *burnout*. She had felt scorched and with-ered, like a tree caught in a summer fire.

And now her cheeks were burning as Vance's cool blue eyes gazed at her calmly. Nothing in his expression or body language even hinted that he was in playboy mode. And anyway, why would he be wanting to play with some-one like *her*? She had seen the photos of some of the women he had dated, with their perfect features and haute couture.

Some of their handbags had cost more than her monthly salary…

No, she was definitely not his type. All Vance was doing was engaging in a kind act for a guest whom he had caught being upset and in tears over something…and he had considered the fact that she wouldn't want to face a lot of people after that.

Nevertheless, she still felt awkward. He wasn't just *anybody*.

"I usually eat breakfast alone," she said, eyes fixed on the menu. Her words came out more gruffly than she had intended. "In fact, I had almost changed my mind about taking this cruise. I just wanted a holiday where I could relax and be pampered and not have to deal with socializing."

She looked up to see Vance gazing at her quizzically. "You can relax and be pampered here. After breakfast, I can introduce you to our spa professionals..."

Chanelle felt the temperature in her cheeks climbing a few notches at the image that flashed in her mind: Vance lying on a spa bed with hot lava stones positioned down his strong, muscled back. And his Aquarius tattoo on the upper right side...

"Um, thanks, but I'll be fine." Besides, her budget had been stretched far enough. She looked around. The view was stupendous. Endless sea and sky. The clouds had shifted, and the sky was a mix of blues with the occasional ribbon of pink.

Vance had been saying something, but *what*? She looked at him blankly. Her stomach did a flip.

"Coffee or tea?" he repeated.

"Sorry…" She held up her hand. "I don't think I should be here." She bit her lip. "I should go." She caught his frown as she began to rise and then promptly sat down again. She owed him an explanation, at the very least. Her heart thumping, she looked at him squarely. Why be anything but honest? "I have to admit I'm feeling a little out of my element," she said. She glanced toward the other guests before turning her gaze back to Vance.

He leaned forward, both elbows on the table and his hands clasped under his chin. "I think you have all the right elements," he said lightly. "And if you're referring to your bank account, it's not an issue, remember? I'm pretty sure I can cover it, unless you're intending to eat me out of house and home. Or should I say ship and stern?" His mouth quirked to reveal a flash of dimple.

"I—I'm…well…*okay*," she relented. Why

was she making such a big deal about the whole thing? She needed to take her own earlier advice and lighten up. "I have to warn you, though," she said, managing a tentative smile, "I do have a good appetite."

Vance nodded his approval as he handed her the menu. "Good. Go crazy. I'm ordering my favorite—buttermilk applesauce pancakes with Ontario maple syrup." He grinned. "Something sweet for a sweet Canadian boy."

Chanelle felt laughter bubble up inside her. She sensed that something was shifting between them. Or maybe it was just *her*. Maybe some of her inhibitions were losing their grip on her. Perhaps it was time to let go of her tendency to control the situation and just enjoy the moment...

She had read enough to know that letting go completely could be a challenge for highly sensitive people like herself. Well, she would rise to the challenge, she decided. Why not enjoy this unexpected turn of events instead of being overwhelmed and feeling out of place? How often would she get the chance to be in the company of a gorgeous guy in a fabulous restaurant on the top deck of his cruise ship? A guy with a dimpled smile that made her stomach swirl in a good way…

"I'll try the crepes filled with hazelnut chocolate and ricotta cheese," she said decisively. "For a sweeter Canadian girl."

He burst out laughing, his eyes crinkling at the edges. "So the Sagittarian has a competitive streak, does she?"

For timeless moments, Chanelle felt like she was suspended in a cloud of pure pleasure as they exchanged smiles. Then the waiter appeared with a carafe of coffee, took their order and reassured them it would be ready shortly.

"So where does this sweeter Canadian girl live?" Vance said, pouring her coffee first.

"Sault Ste. Marie, Ontario," she replied, adding cream to her cup.

He nodded. "Ah, the Soo. Been there. Stopped overnight on my way to Lake Superior for a fishing trip with some guys—let me see—three years ago. Nice little town. Big Italian population, right?"

Chanelle nodded, taken aback that he had come through her hometown.

"We stayed at a hotel by Saint Mary's River. Checked out the Station Mall; one of our absentminded buddies had brought all his fishing gear but had forgotten the important stuff, like clothes and underwear." He chuckled. "While he went searching for his designer boxers, the rest of us waited it out at a pizza and gelato place." He sighed. "I ordered a double scoop of hazelnut and pistachio. *Heaven.*"

Her eyes widened. "You've got a great memory."

He looked at her unblinkingly. "I remember anything that looks good and tastes even better," he said, his mouth tilting up at one corner.

Chanelle felt a warm rush swish through her. Flustered, she looked down and took a sip of her coffee. Her mind was zooming to places she didn't want it to go, and she'd be horrified if Vance even suspected what she was conjuring up in her imagination...

"So after Pete was done, we spent a few hours at the casino, then had some amazing Italian food at the Marconi Club." He chuckled. "*Mamma mia*, just the memory of it is making my mouth water. I'd go back to the Soo again just for the food. Although—" he raised an eyebrow conspiratorially "—I suspect the people are just as appealing..."

Chanelle raised her chin. "Yes, we are. And the Soo is a great place to live. Not too big, not too small. I don't know if I could ever live in a huge city like Toronto or Vancouver. Mind you, I visited Toronto a few years ago. I actually went on a weekend bus tour with a couple of my friends to catch a show at the Princess of Wales Theatre. It was a long trip, though. Eight hours or so."

"So you've been to my hometown. We have great Italian food, too." He grinned. "And every other cuisine you can think of."

"Do you love it? Living in a huge city, I mean?"

"I enjoy all the big-city perks, but I do need the occasional getaway."

"Where do you get away to?" Chanelle asked casually. "Other than Lake Superior."

"British Columbia, Newfoundland, California, the Caribbean…usually a place where there's a large body of water," he said with a laugh. "Do you have any special places you like to escape to?"

"I've stayed pretty much close to home," she said sheepishly. "Worked a lot of overtime hours… But I do have some special spots in and around the Soo. A beautiful beach called Pointe des Chenes. And I've camped up north, Lake Superior way. Batchawana Bay, Pancake Bay. I'm a northern Ontario girl. Love my lakes and forests."

Vance was staring at her with an intensity that made her breath catch in her lungs. *He's genuinely interested in what I'm saying*, she thought in wonder.

The waiter returned with their orders. Chanelle took a first bite of her crepe and closed her eyes. "Heaven," she murmured, before realizing she had used the same term Vance had used to describe his gelato.

"Of course it is." He nodded. "It's the *nocciola*."

Hazelnut. Of course. Her workplace was on Queen Street East, within walking distance to the Station Mall, and she often had lunch at one of the eateries there, ending it occasionally with a gelato at the same place he had been to.

"So we share the same taste in Italian ice cream." Vance drizzled syrup over his pancakes and cut a wedge. "Delicious," he said, and slid the plate closer to her. "Want to try?"

The familiarity with which he spoke made

Chanelle's pulse skip. "That's okay, thanks. I think I have more than enough on my plate." Her fork paused in midair. "Literally and figuratively."

Vance looked at her thoughtfully. "Are you thinking you might go back to the same job?"

Chanelle swallowed. "I'm not sure. I loved my job." She heard the defensive tone in her voice.

Vance poured more syrup on his second pancake. "What made you decide to get into social work?"

Chanelle looked down at her half-eaten crepe and tapped it mindlessly with her fork. "I spent my childhood without a father," she said, "and I became self-conscious when there were events at school where parents were invited. My mother came when she could, but most times, it was too hard for her. She was working two jobs to pay the bills. My grandfather had health issues, so he and my grandma couldn't always be there, either." She looked up. "I think subconsciously, I internalized the fact that my father had denied my existence. Even before my mother told me that he had taken off before I was born, I intuitively felt my father's abandonment." She paused, expecting to see a skeptical look in Vance's eyes, but what she saw were his furrowed brows and eyes narrowed in concern.

"I know now that having a sharper intuition is characteristic of a highly sensitive person. Which is why, I believe, I knew early in life that I wanted to help others, starting with my mother. I felt her pain, even though she tried to put up a good front. So I helped around the house without being told, was a high achiever at school, did everything possible to avoid making life harder for her." She gazed away from Vance, recalling how happy she had been when her mother eventually married her stepdad. On the other hand, her unresolved feelings about her biological father had continued to intensify over the years, and she had felt lingering hurt and resentment that he hadn't valued her from the moment he'd known she existed, hadn't deemed her worthy to claim her as his daughter.

Parker's breaking off their engagement and leaving had ignited similar feelings...

Stop thinking about Parker, she chided herself. *He's not worth it.* She turned her gaze back to Vance, who was still looking at her with an intensity that made her heart twinge, but not in a hurtful way.

"I'm sorry, I'm sure you don't want to hear me keep chattering incessantly."

"Don't be sorry, Chanelle. It's obvious that your caring personality growing up under challenging circumstances was a good indication that you'd eventually choose a helping profession."

"Some kids had it worse than I did. One of my classmates came to school with bruises on her arms and face one Friday. I felt so bad for her. She had moved to town about a couple of months earlier, and we were getting to be good friends."

Chanelle gave a shiver. "Kayla had parents, but the rumor was that they were drug addicts. She told the teacher that she had fallen down some stairs, and she was quiet all day. She didn't tell me anything. The teacher told the principal, and on Monday, Kayla didn't show up." They had been in grade nine, and the defeated look she had seen in Kayla's eyes had haunted her all weekend.

Chanelle drew in a deep breath. "We found

out that Children's Aid had investigated and removed Kayla from her home immediately. Fortunately, she had a caring aunt out of town who took her in." Chanelle couldn't keep her eyes from blurring. She wiped at them hastily with her napkin. "I knew then that I wanted to become a social worker so I could protect children from abusive or neglectful family members." She sniffed. "I never saw Kayla again, but I have something she had given me for Kris Kringle." Chanelle extended her arm to show Vance the bracelet around her left wrist that Kayla had woven with a variety of colorful threads.

"You've kept it all these years?" Vance looked at her incredulously.

Chanelle nodded. "I became a child protection worker because of her." She smiled. "I don't usually wear it around the clock, only when I'm at work. You could say it's my Sagittarian quiver, loaded with arrows. I know it may sound silly, but wearing the bracelet makes me feel strong, makes me believe that I have the protection I need, especially when I have to rescue kids."

"Wow," he said huskily, shaking his head.

"Wow." He reached out to take her hand and stroked the bracelet thoughtfully with his thumb. "It's not silly at all, Chanelle." Suddenly his other hand closed over hers as well. Chanelle's heart flipped and started thumping so hard she missed most of what Vance was saying next.

Her stupefied look must have clued him in. "You're stronger than you think," he repeated, his eyes narrowing. He withdrew his hands as the waiter appeared, asking them if he could take any plates away.

They both nodded, and when the waiter was gone, Chanelle gave a big sigh. "I'm hoping that while I'm on the cruise, wearing the bracelet will help me decide where to go from here..." She let her gaze drift beyond Vance to the sky, now a deep azure that seemed to be an extension of his eyes. "But right now, I just can't see myself in another job."

"Give yourself time, Chanelle," he murmured. "You'll know when the time is right... So while you're on this cruise, I want you to give yourself permission to relax and have fun. Live a little. You deserve it." He stood up. "Starting now. Captain's—no, president's orders. Got it?" He looked at her sternly then flashed her another one of his ridiculously gorgeous brighter-than-sunshine smiles.

Chanelle pulled her chair back and rose. "Got it," she said, flinging her hair back. "I'd hate to disobey and end up walking the plank."

He burst out laughing. "Are you implying, fair lass, that I have the black heart of a pirate?"

Chanelle's pulse vaulted, his words and hearty laugh evoking an image of him in full pirate regalia standing on the bow of a treasure ship, one eye covered by a black patch, the other pinning her with the same crystal clarity as the turquoise waters below.

She couldn't stop the corners of her mouth from lifting. "If not a pirate, then perhaps a scallywag," she said, feigning haughtiness. And flipping her hair back, she strode off toward the exit.

After Chanelle disappeared, leaving him dazed with the memory of her flashing eyes and pixy smile, Vance checked in on his mother, Mariah and Adrien, and then returned to his stateroom to try to sort out some issues that were playing around in his mind as well as the jumble of emotions Chanelle had activated in his gut.

Some of the details that Chanelle had shared about her life had disturbed him. His gaze had been riveted to the shifting emotions on her face as she'd told him about her father abandoning her and her mother's challenges raising her, and he had felt his stomach twist at the difficulties she had experienced. And when she had teared up about Kayla, he had felt a strong urge to wrap his arms around her and hold her head against him.

Her impish smile as she strode off after implying he was a scallywag had caused a different feeling in him—a hammering in his chest that had reverberated throughout his body...

Now, stretched out on the recliner on his balcony, Vance thought again of Chanelle's early years growing up without a father. His own father had been present only minimally, so he could just imagine what Chanelle had felt, especially being so sensitive.

Vance's memory shifted to how he had immersed himself in a new and heavily structured routine after his father had passed. This week—with nothing specifically planned except for the midweek gala—was throwing him off. He might have been more laid-back when it came to work in the past, but that had changed dramatically in the last nine months. He had conditioned himself to get up at 5:00 a.m. every morning, work out at the gym in his condo, shower, have breakfast and be at the office before eight. And most nights, he wasn't back at his condo until after nine.

He'd had no time to think about women.

Until yesterday, after seeing an auburn-haired beauty trying to rescue his nephew from danger.

And after spending some time with Chanelle Robinson in the Mezza Luna Ristorante, and foolishly inviting her to have breakfast with him in the Constellation Club this morning, he was now in danger of losing his resolve to focus on work, not women. Or more specifically, *this* woman.

Vance pursed his lips. He would be on this cruise for three more days after today. And when the cruise was over, he'd never see Chanelle Robinson again. He might not even run into her for the remainder of the cruise.

The important thing to remember was not to

seek her out. It would only weaken his resolve. So despite the undeniable way his senses were stirred around her, he had to ensure that he did not act on his feelings. How could he take advantage of her in the vulnerable state she was in, having suffered a broken relationship and work stress?

You've changed, big boy, whether you like it or not.

He froze at the words that had shoved their way into his consciousness. They were true. Before his father died, Vance had never suffered pangs of guilt around relationships, familial or otherwise. He had justified his rebelliousness as a teen and young adult as his way of striking out at a father who was never home. A father who seemed to care more about work than his kids...

The feeling of guilt had sprung up when his father died, knowing he had allowed his built-up resentment to stop him from granting his dad's dying request. Since then, he had been trying to make up for it.

Yes, he had changed, all right.

He had made work his priority, just as his father had done, and slowly, Vance had begun to understand how a person could become consumed with work, with passion, to the point of neglecting everything else.

He could congratulate himself for repressing his playboy ways while focusing on carrying out his father's last wish, but he couldn't deny that certain feelings had been reactivated.

By a fascinating woman who probably wanted nothing to do with him or any other man right now...

But it wasn't just her outer beauty that attracted him. He was intrigued by the depth of her character, her small-town charm and honesty. Her devotion to her job, the children she was so passionate about protecting. Her goodness.

And how could he not be affected by those limpid green pools for eyes, those peachy cheekbones and silky lips? How could he ignore the sleek curves of her body...and that riotous head of hair that he envisioned blowing in the wind as she stood on a rocky outcrop looking out at the endless ice-blue waters of Lake Superior? A Sagittarian warrior, softhearted yet strong and determined, ready to fling her Archer's arrow...

A thought entered his consciousness, shocking him like his very first dip in Lake Superior. He was falling for Chanelle Robinson.

Falling hard and seeing stars...

CHAPTER EIGHT

CHANELLE HAD WATCHED Vance leave in a swirl of emotions. She had felt some undercurrents in Vance's presence…undercurrents that confused her. Like the intensity in his gaze earlier in the elevator. It had only lasted for a couple of seconds, but the expression in his electric-blue eyes as he looked down at her had galvanized her to the core. And then minutes later, in the Constellation Club, his expression had been genuinely reassuring, making her doubt her earlier assessment.

But the way he had been so attentive, fixing her with that enigmatic gaze, was causing uncertainty in the pit of her stomach about his true feelings.

What true feelings? an inner voice scoffed. *You just met the guy. Do you actually think he has feelings for you? And if you're feeling anything for him, it's because he's gorgeous and rich. And what's wrong with that?*

Chanelle scowled. Yes, how could she not find Vance Kingston attractive? Very attractive. The memory of the Aquarius tattoo on his muscled back made her catch her breath. But it hadn't been thoughts of his wealth that had generated flutters in her chest, that had sent tingles to every part of her. It was the way he had given her all his attention, as if her every word mattered to him. It was how he had validated her by listening to her story, acknowledging her strength, showing concern for her work situation and encouraging her to give it time and to have fun on the cruise.

She couldn't dispute the fact that Vance Kingston was gorgeous and rich. He had asked her to join him for breakfast and he had shown himself to be considerate and thoughtful. But it was just plain silly to think that the president of Zodiac Cruises was at all interested in her in any other way.

And even if he *was* taking a break from his playboy lifestyle for the sake of work—if the articles online were true—Chanelle couldn't imagine someone like him changing his ways after his self-imposed period of solitude.

She shook her head impatiently. Vance had

taken up enough of her head space. She was here to relax and enjoy the cruise, just as he had suggested, and not to waste time fantasizing about him or any other man.

Chanelle focused her attention on the Star Guide, an interactive screen that displayed a map of the entire ship and the features on every deck. She decided on a visit to the art gallery on Deck Five. The stunning art collection would be a welcome distraction from her thoughts of Vance Kingston.

There were dozens of international artists featured, not only in the gallery itself, but displayed along the walls on each deck. Chanelle spent close to an hour marveling at the diversity of styles, the vibrancy of the colors and the intricacy and detail in each painting. One particularly captivated her, with its depiction of a moonlit and starry sky mirrored in the indigo-blue undulations of the sea. It was called *Enchantment*, and simply signed *SV.*

A glance at the price made Chanelle's eyes widen. A fairy godmother would have to appear and sprinkle some magic fairy dust in Chanelle's wallet for her to be able to afford it.

Chanelle picked up a complimentary booklet showcasing the artists and their works but couldn't find anything about the artist and his or her painting. An elegantly dressed woman sitting at an ornate French Provincial desk walked over with a smile and told Chanelle that the artist wished to remain anonymous. She gave Chanelle a card with information about the champagne art auction that would be taking place during the mid-cruise gala, and explained that there would be many more pieces featured. And complimentary champagne, of course, a door prize, and some special surprises...

Chanelle slipped the invitation into her handbag and smiled her thanks at the woman before moving on. It sounded like fun, but she doubted that there would be a painting that her budget could accommodate.

Chanelle slowed her pace as she entered the Galaxy Shops. She had splurged on booking the cruise itself and had vowed to be strict with herself when it came to shopping, whether on the ship or during her off-ship excursion. But there was no harm in just looking, she told herself, surveying the luxurious brands of purses and luggage. She checked the price of a coral clutch that caught her eye and sighed before moving on to the jewelry displays. One of the sales staff approached her with a welcoming smile, telling her about the day's special of fifty percent off select brands. Chanelle thanked her, flushing, and told her that she'd have a good look. Which wasn't exactly lying. She *would* look through the sparkly selection.

A pair of ruby earrings in a flower design caught her eye. She noticed the price, then began to walk away. How could she justify spending money unnecessarily, especially when she wasn't one hundred percent sure that she would be returning to her job in a month's time? How was she supposed to recover from five years of intensive work stress in one month? And then what? Would she be ready to get right back into it?

She had rent to pay. And now that she was back on her own, she might even have to look for a new place...or move back in with her mom and stepdad.

Not that she didn't love them, but it would be hard after five years of independence in her own space.

"I'll take these amethyst earrings, dear," a

woman said close by. "I think they'll match my violet gown perfectly for the gala."

Chanelle turned and saw a sixty-something woman sporting a smart pixie cut with side-swept bangs that suited her silver-gray hair. She was wearing turquoise palazzo pants and a sleeveless ivory chiffon top. She had removed her turquoise earrings to try the amethyst ones against her ears. On the third finger of her left hand, an enormous diamond sparkled under the ceiling lights.

The woman's open handbag slipped off the counter, spilling some of its contents. Chanelle quickly bent down to retrieve what she could and handed the items to the woman, who gazed across at her with a grateful smile. "Thanks for your help."

"My pleasure," she replied, startled by the crystal clarity of the woman's blue eyes.

Chanelle was about to stand up, too, but a flash on the floor under the counter caught her eye. It was a photo of a child, encased in a plastic folder. A boy with the same arresting blue eyes as the woman.

And the president of Zodiac Cruises.

Something fluttered in Chanelle's chest as

she stood up and handed the photo of the little boy she had tried to rescue yesterday to his grandmother. *Vance Kingston's mother...*

No wonder Chanelle had sensed something familiar about her.

After the woman left, Chanelle returned to the jewelry display to look at the ruby earrings. A new voice was telling her, *Relax and have fun. Live a little. You deserve it!*

Foolish or not, Chanelle listened to the voice. Which, she realized as she walked away with her little velvet box tucked away in a Zodiac Cruises gift bag, was the voice of Vance Kingston.

Vance looked over the series of sketches he had been working on for the last hour. There were at least a dozen variations of the logo he was designing for the new cruise line in the Zodiac fleet, its first ship scheduled to launch the following year. His father had initiated the project, and now it was in his hands.

He had to come up with a new name as well, and he had jotted down a half dozen possibilities, including Nebula Cruises, What's Your Sign? Cruises and Stellar Cruises. None of them quite clicked for him, though. He pursed his lips. The logos all had one thing in common—undulating waves. Once he decided on a name, he'd connect the letters with the waves in a flowing forward motion. And maybe add the profile of a sea goddess...

Vance turned to a new page and started another sketch. It was neither a logo nor a name. It was a face with sculpted cheekbones and full, curving lips. Eyes framed with long, feathery lashes. And thick waves of hair cascading down to the shoulder lines.

He took a green and a gold pencil and added color to the eyes. He set his pencils down and took a long, hard look at the result.

Chanelle Robinson was staring back at him...

Time to take a break, he told himself, shaking his head in wonder.

Vance greeted the art representative at her desk and strolled through the gallery, noticing the new paintings that had been added. Vance enjoyed perusing each one, familiar with many of the artists. He was looking forward to the champagne art auction and wondered if Chanelle planned to attend.

He stopped when he came to the *Enchantment* painting and looked at it thoughtfully.

"It's getting some attention," the art rep said as she joined him.

"Oh?" Vance's eyebrows lifted. "Did someone ask about it, Stephanie?"

"A young lady kept going back to it. She must have stared at it for a good ten minutes." Stephanie smiled at Vance. "She was obviously enchanted by it."

Vance's mouth curved. "But not enchanted enough to buy it," he chuckled.

"Well, perhaps she might consider it at the auction on gala night, Vance. I gave her a card."

"Was she one of our regular cruisers?" Stephanie had been with the *Aquarius* since it launched, and she had become familiar with returning customers, especially the art patrons.

"No, this was a first-timer," she told him. A few guests entered the gallery, and she turned toward them.

"Did you happen to catch her name?" Vance said as casually as he could.

Stephanie looked back. "I spotted her first name on her lanyard. It was different; it reminded me of Chantilly lace." She laughed.

"Chantelle. No, *Chanelle.*" She walked over and welcomed the guests, and Vance turned back to gaze at the painting.

Enchantment. Why had this painting caught Chanelle's attention? he mused. His gaze swooped over the stars and the waves of blue and indigo before landing on the initials in the bottom right-hand corner. *SV.* His mouth lifted at one corner. He had done this painting while he was working on his masters of fine art degree, and not wanting his father to denigrate it on the rare occasions when he came home, Vance had chosen not to sign it with his own name. He had to thank his sister for giving him the nickname Sir Vancelot...

CHAPTER NINE

CHANELLE PUT ON a light robe and drew the tie around her waist. She had returned to her stateroom feeling overwhelmed at bumping into Vance's mother—and overheated after spending time in the shop—and had immediately taken a refreshing shower.

She inhaled and exhaled deeply, feeling much more relaxed now, and headed to the balcony. She could stare at the water for ages, watching the cerulean waves change to turquoise and turquoise to cobalt blue. The sun was adding magic to the scene, making the water's surface shimmer with glittering diamonds.

In the next few weeks, she hoped it would be clearer to her what direction to take as far as her job was concerned. This cruise would hopefully give both her body and mind a rest, and then she could decide if she could handle continuing in the same line of work, or if she seriously needed to consider a change of some kind.

But now she didn't really want to think about it. She just wanted to enjoy the glorious view of sky and sea.

Chanelle went back inside and stretched out on top of the bed. She checked the time on her phone. Plenty of time to relax before dinner.

She reached for the daily cruise guide, and while she was checking out the featured events of the day, the daily horoscope caught her eye. She couldn't help skimming the page until her gaze landed on her sign.

Sagittarius, you're in for some surprises. With your ruler Jupiter in retrograde, your inner world is transitioning and spinning you to a higher consciousness. Don't fight it; let yourself enjoy your burgeoning awareness. You may have felt the universe is not on your side after some personal and work upsets, but take heart, Sag. If you stay focused on what's in front of you, what's to come won't be problematic. Go with the flow, Archer, and that arrow will land where it needs to…

* * *

Chanelle frowned. It was so *eerie* how much the words could be applied to her situation. And then she scoffed at herself. Parts of the description could apply to tons of people, no matter what their sign was.

Despite her skepticism, she couldn't help reading the horoscope for Vance.

The stars will collaborate to help a business matter come to fruition. Complicated family issues will untangle, and with Uranus guiding you, you will be able to see clearer when it comes to matters of the heart. Concessions may need to be made, and your compliance with the forces of the universe will result in a shower of positive changes.

Chanelle set down the guide and let her gaze drift to the ceiling. Could Vance, despite his calm and collected exterior, have some personal issues of his own he was dealing with? A woman who was waiting for him to ease up at work and shower her with more of his attention?

She shook her head. What was she doing conjuring up possibilities around Vance and his relationships?

Time to get back to reality.

She picked up the guide again. A glance at the time confirmed that she had a few free hours before dinner. Did she really want to spend them lying down on her bed? She was on a spectacular cruise ship and before she knew it, it would be over...

She might as well enjoy every delicious bit of it.

Chanelle perused the activities listed for the afternoon: a tour of the ship kitchens, a magic show featuring a Las Vegas regular, an art class with a high-profile artist, a wine-tasting class, Latin dancing or belly-dancing instruction, a rock-climbing wall, a pool volleyball tournament, a '70s disco party and a dozen other choices.

Chanelle began to reread the list, the times and the locations. She didn't really feel up to doing anything that required dressing up; after all, she'd be doing that for Canada Night. But she really should consider doing something a little out of her element. After all, what would be the likelihood of her going on another cruise any time soon? She might as well try something new. *And exciting...*

As she skimmed down the list, her gaze landed on something that she had missed. The Sky Promenade. It was an extensive course of colorful horizontal rope ladders that were suspended a hundred feet above the skating rink on the top deck, connecting to rope bridges, slopes and descents that had to be navigated by walking while wearing a safety harness.

Chanelle flicked on to the TV channel that featured videos of all the day's events. As the Sky Promenade video started, she gave a little shiver. Heights had always made her feel a little queasy, and this activity would require a stomach of steel, looking down between the ropes to the crystal-clear surface of the ice rink.

There was no way she could do that. No. Way.

She'd be terrified, even knowing that she'd be wearing a safety harness. The motion of the ropes along with the bird's-eye view of the sea on the periphery would throw her off balance with her first step. She clicked off the remote. There had to be something else she could try that wasn't so scary.

Chanelle leaped off the bed and changed into

a pair of purple leggings and a thigh-length fuchsia T-shirt before tying her hair up in a ponytail. She'd do something outdoors, she decided, but something less extreme. Perhaps she could try the rock-climbing wall…

Vance's cell phone buzzed, making him start. It was Mariah, reminding him that he'd promised to take Adrien swimming. He checked the time. He'd also planned a quick meeting with the director of environmental operations later in the afternoon for an update on her latest initiative. He smirked. He was supposed to be taking a break from work while on the cruise, but he was realizing just how hard it was to break an established habit…

And after the meeting, he would join Mariah, Adrien and his mother for dinner in the Galaxy Café. Tonight was Canada Night on the ship. The theater would be featuring Canadian singers and comedians, and the Galaxy Café would be serving a signature dish and dessert from every province. There would be wine from the vineyards of the Okanagan Valley in British Columbia and Ontario's Niagara region, cheeses from Quebec, seafood from off the

Pacific and Atlantic coasts, organic breads from the Prairies, and more. And sweets galore, like Nanaimo bars, butter tarts and *tarte au sucre*, three of his favorites.

Those who wanted to experience a Canadian winter would have the option of skating on an outdoor ice rink located on the top deck on the opposite side of the Constellation Club. It would be lit up after dark, and there would be blowers blowing in soft imitation snowflakes. And there would be hot chocolate stations and beaver tail pastries made and served on the spot. It couldn't get more Canadian than that.

Vance smiled. The deep-fried pastry, shaped like a beaver tail and topped with anything from cinnamon and sugar to whipped cream and hazelnut chocolate spread, was something he always enjoyed after skating on Ottawa's Rideau Canal, one of Canada's iconic landmarks. There were thousands of skaters and always a line for the beaver tails.

As he changed into swim trunks and a white cotton T-shirt, Vance couldn't help wondering what Chanelle was doing now, and where she would be dining this evening.

Playing volleyball with Adrien in the pool gave Vance a feeling of lightness that he hadn't felt in a long time. Along with a twinge of guilt. He had neglected his godfather duties these past months, and he had missed this. Having fun with a kid. A special kid, who had stolen his heart from the moment Vance had seen his pink and puckered little face in the hospital.

Mariah had asked him if he would be the child's godfather.

"Hell, yes," he had blurted, and then, more cautiously, "Does that mean I have to change diapers?"

"That's part of the deal, Sir Vancelot," she had replied with a shake of her head. "Don't worry, we'll have you practicing on a regular basis. You'll be a pro by the time you have one or nine of your own." Vance had feigned looking horrified, and Mariah and her husband, Chris, had burst out laughing.

Mariah had been true to her word. Adrien had gotten used to Vance being around from the very beginning, and whenever Chris was out of town on business—which was often, since he was the head of a mining engineering company that had projects all over the globe—Vance had gladly stepped up his godfather duties.

Enjoying double-scoop ice cream cones after their swim, Vance felt a contentment that had eluded him after his father had died. He realized that a part of him—maybe a big part of him—had shut down. The part that was all about the enjoyment of simple things, like splashing around a pool and having a cone with his nephew.

But he was determined to change his routine of the past nine months. He would spend more time with Adrien.

And maybe it was time to make some other changes, too...

Vance felt a thrumming in his chest as an image of Chanelle broke through his thoughts.

A coil of desire skimmed through his veins at the memory of her lying on the chaise lounge with that mint-green swimsuit clinging to her body like a second skin.

Yes, he needed to make some changes.

Starting with bringing Adrien back and then seeing if he could find Chanelle.

* * *

A flash of pink and purple caught his eye as he leaped up the open stairway to the top deck. From this center point, he could see a number of people clambering up the rock-climbing wall, and a line of others waiting for their turn. The pink and purple lady at the end of the line had auburn hair tied up in a ponytail.

Could it be Chanelle?

She turned slightly, and Vance's pulse leaped. It *was* her. He strode toward her, a strange wave of happiness washing over him. He had decided on a whim to start looking for Chanelle on the top deck and work his way down. Maybe this was a sign...

"Hey, miss," he called, just steps behind her.

She whirled around, her ponytail flicking him sharply across the chin. "Oh, sorry," she said, her eyes widening. "Didn't mean to strike, but you kinda crept up on me."

"There you go, insinuating that I'm a creep again," he said, smiling at her crookedly.

Chanelle's eyelashes fluttered, and her mouth opened defensively. "And there *you* go, putting words in my mouth again."

An electric tingle radiated through Vance at

the teasing tone of her words. He gazed at her wordlessly for a few moments, unable to draw his eyes away from the gleaming hazel green of hers.

Finally the line shifted as another rock climber began his ascent. "So is this your first time?" he said, gesturing toward the wall.

"Yes, I've mustered up the courage to try something new on this cruise," she said with a chuckle. "I considered the Sky Promenade, but after watching the video, I decided to leave that to the daredevils."

"Hmm." He surveyed her thoughtfully. "Are you afraid of heights?"

"Well…" She turned to scan the extensive series of ropes positioned above the skating rink at one far end of the ship. "I'm afraid that with *my* luck, *I'll* be the one whose safety harness breaks."

"Not gonna happen," he said, shaking his head. "I think, Miss Robinson, that there are some trust issues here that we have to deal with." The line moved forward again, leaving two more people waiting in front of Chanelle. "Come on, let me show you that you can do this. Conquer your fear, put your trust in the universe…"

"The universe isn't going to catch me if I fall," she retorted.

"But *I* will." He heard the words jump out of his mouth. "Look, Chanelle, you don't even have to worry about me catching you, because you won't fall. Safety is our number-one priority onboard this ship. Trust me."

Vance saw her forehead crease. "Okay, here's the deal. I haven't actually tried the rope walk myself. And to tell you the truth," he murmured, leaning forward as if to share a secret he didn't want anyone to hear, "*I'm* not exactly crazy about heights. I'm a water guy, remember?" He patted himself on the back, where he had the Aquarius symbol tattooed. "So how about we both try something new and scary together?"

Chanelle was gaping at him as if he were delusional. "You've got to be kidding." She was momentarily distracted as the person in front of her went to get fitted with her safety harness. She turned back to Vance. "You're *not* kidding."

Vance grinned. "Come on, Chanelle. It's now

or never. If you can do *this*, you can do anything."

Chanelle blinked at him. Then her gaze
shifted upward to the Sky Promenade.

She took a deep breath and slowly exhaled,
her eyes meeting his again. "Fine," she declared. "Lead the way!"

From her platform, strapped into her safety
harness, Chanelle scanned the view around her
with a fluttering in her stomach that continued
downward into her legs. The sky was a calm
blue with the occasional fluffy cloud drifting
nonchalantly by. The sea below was a deeper
blue and not as calm, the froth of whitecaps
disappearing and reappearing with every un-
dulation. Lined against the side of the ship was
a series of lifeboats. Chanelle breathed in and
out slowly, hoping she wouldn't hyperventilate.

What on earth had made her agree to this?

Her gaze shifted to the colorful system of
thick rungs that resembled a giant crocheted
doily suspended above the ice rink. Each
stretch of ladder led to a post with a circular
platform where you stopped and gathered your
courage before attempting the next rope ladder.

Some ladders were horizontal, some slightly vertical, with vertical ropes suspended on either side.

Chanelle held her breath as Vance took his first step. She watched the rope ladder swing with his every movement, and she gasped when his foot seemed to be slipping. And then Vance gingerly made his way across the next half dozen rungs before stepping onto the circular platform and turning around to give her a thumbs-up sign.

Chanelle looked above to the metal track into which her safety rope was inserted, so she could glide along as she maneuvered the swinging steps. She could either cling to this rope, which was attached to her body harness, or grasp the cord dangling on either side of her to help her keep her balance.

Why am I doing this? she asked herself again. Vance had encouraged her to conquer her fear, put her trust in the universe...to trust him.

Perhaps she *did* have trust issues, as he had suggested. Maybe deep down she was afraid that history would repeat itself when it came to men, and that whoever came into her life would eventually abandon her... Maybe she was afraid of letting go of her job and trying something new. Maybe she was afraid of letting go of the HSP safety net that kept her cautious and protected.

But maybe it also kept her from experiencing life fully. When had she last felt adrenaline pumping in her veins like right now? Yes, she was afraid, about to step out onto the rope ladder, but she felt an exhilaration at the thought of doing it anyway. She looked across at Vance, who nodded at her with a confident smile and gave her another thumbs-up.

With her heart clanging against her ribs, Chanelle clasped the vertical ropes on either side of her and planted her foot on the first rung. The view below her made her knees tremble. She forced herself to focus on the rung, and gripping the ropes even harder, she put her left foot forward.

The sway of the ladder made her give a yelp. There was no way she could continue…

"You can do it, Chanelle."

Vance's calm voice reached her, and her head snapped up to look at him. His expression was just as calm, as if he knew that that was what she needed instead of a loud exhortation or cheer.

She had to believe that the harness wouldn't let go, that she wouldn't plummet to the ice rink. *Trust me*, Vance had said.

With whatever ounce of courage that still remained in her, Chanelle wobbled across the ladder and stepped up on the platform and into Vance's arms.

Vance tightened his arms around her. "I knew you could do it," he murmured close to her ear. Chest to chest, the heightened pumping of his heart—and hers—made him wish they were alone somewhere so he could savor the sensation that was flooding him.

He felt something primal, instinctive...a desire to protect this woman who had been brave enough to go against her own natural instincts and put her trust in the universe. *In him*. And the way she was clinging to him made him wonder if she could sense his feelings.

Out of the corner of his eye, he could see the attendant waiting for him and Chanelle to proceed before allowing the next guest to take a step forward. There were still plenty of ladders and bridges to navigate. They had to move on.

"Okay, Chanelle, one step at a time. Ready?"

She looked up at him, and his heart swelled at the look in the misty green depths of her eyes. This was not going to be easy for him, either. He would rather be in the pool than up in the air. Taking a deep breath, he released his arms around Chanelle and grasped the vertical ropes. "I'll be waiting for you," he told her huskily before stepping forward.

With open arms.

"My legs feel wobbly," Chanelle said as they left the Sky Promenade. "In fact, I feel wobbly all over…"

Vance nodded. "Join the club. It's the adrenaline rush." He put his hand under her elbow. "How about we sit down for a few minutes with a nice refreshing drink?"

"No alcohol for me," Chanelle protested. "That would finish me off. You'd have to carry me the rest of the way."

"I meant something fruity. Like a tall, cool glass of freshly squeezed lemonade. Or a mango-peach power drink. And by the way,

Chanelle," he added with a grin, "my knees are wobbly, too, but not too wobbly to carry a Sagittarius warrior." He raised a hand to give her a high five. "You killed it up there."

She lifted her chin. "I did, didn't I?" She gave a little laugh. "So yes, I'll let you buy me a drink. Mango-peach sounds yummy."

"Mmm. I don't recall offering to foot the bill. But since I'm such a chivalrous guy, I'll do the chivalrous thing. *This time.*"

"Thank you, *Sir Vancelot.*" She beamed at him. "And by the way…you killed it up there, too!"

CHAPTER TEN

CHANELLE WANTED SOMETHING a little more dressy for Canada Night. The captain of *Aquarius* and some of the senior officers and staff would be greeting guests on Deck Five from eight to nine, and those who wished could have their professional photo taken with the captain during the last half hour. Not that *she* was interested in a photo...

Stop kidding yourself, an inner voice taunted. *You may not be interested in meeting the captain of Aquarius or getting a photo, but there will most certainly be a certain Vance Kingston there to impress...*

Did she want to impress him?

Maybe, a small voice admitted.

Something had happened between them up on the Sky Promenade. She wasn't sure if it was the moment when she had looked across at him on the circular platform, and he had nodded for her to proceed, his eyes as calm and blue as the sky above them. Or when she had made it across the first ladder and had literally sunk into his arms. All she could hear against his chest was his heartbeat along with hers.

She had accomplished a feat she had never thought herself capable of. And she would have never done it without Vance's encouragement. Every step of the way. His arms around her had given her such a wondrous feeling of support.

Or maybe something more...

She felt excited about the evening ahead. She was here on a cruise, and she intended to enjoy as much of it as she could.

Chanelle sifted through her dresses in the closet for something that might go with the Canada Night theme. She stopped when she came to a white cotton dress with splashes of red poppies. Well, they were as close as she could get to the red maple leaf on the Canadian flag. The dress was sleeveless, with a fitted bodice, snazzy red belt and skirt that flared from the waist, reaching to above her knees. And her new ruby earrings matched perfectly. As Chanelle swirled to look at herself in the mirror, she felt like a different person. A care-free, much younger person, without the preoccupations that had clung to her while at work.

Chanelle took a deep breath. She hadn't made much time to go out in the evenings when she had been working. She had usually come home late, exhausted, with thoughts only of getting into a shower and pajamas. Had Parker ever even seen her dressed up like this?

The thought of Parker vanished as quickly as it had come. All she could picture in her mind was the expression she hoped to see on Vance's face when he caught sight of her in this gorgeous dress... She swirled around, loving how the skirt swirled with her. The words of her horoscope came back to her:

Your inner world is transitioning and spinning you to a higher consciousness.

She smiled at herself in the mirror. She was spinning, all right.

And she liked how it felt.

Chanelle chose a black purse that matched the black centers of the poppies, slipped on black high-heeled sandals and headed to the Galaxy Café. She looked forward to enjoying some of the featured dishes—like Digby scallops and other maritime delights—and then she'd make her way to Deck Five.

The place was bustling. As Chanelle looked around for an empty table and didn't see one, she regretted not arriving earlier. Pursing her lips, she considered leaving and trying one of the other dining spots but was blocked by a passing group.

"That's the nice young lady who helped me today," a voice came out of nowhere. "Invite her over, Vance. There's an empty spot at our table."

Through the shifting throng, Chanelle turned and caught sight of Mrs. Kingston, who was smiling directly at her while nudging Vance gently on the arm. Vance's sister and nephew were staring at Chanelle openly, and as Chanelle met Vance's enigmatic gaze, she felt a flush travel up her neck to her cheeks, which she was sure were now as red as the poppies.

"That's the lady who tried to rescue me," Adrien cried, pointing directly at Chanelle.

Chanelle wished there was a way of rescuing herself. She hadn't expected to meet Vance's family, let alone dine with them. Now she had no choice but to wait for Vance to approach. A few moments later, the group had moved on and Vance was striding toward her. Before her eyes met his, Chanelle just managed to scan gray straight-leg trousers that fit impeccably and a baby-blue fitted shirt and a Canadian-themed tie with alternating rows of loons and maple leaves. Under other circumstances, she might have joked about it.

"The Archer—slash—good fairy strikes again," he said, a glint in his blue eyes.

"It happens when I least expect it," she replied, unable to keep a note of defensiveness from creeping into her voice.

Her pulse spiked when Vance cupped her elbow to direct her toward his table. "I believe you've met everyone in my family but haven't been properly introduced to my mother. Chanelle Robinson, Elizabeth Kingston."

"Nice to see you again, Mrs. Kingston." Chanelle noticed that they had started on their meal, but Vance's spot was empty. "I'm sorry to disturb your dinner."

"Please call me Betty." The older woman smiled as they shook hands. "And it's not a disturbance. Is this your first cruise, Chanelle?"

Chanelle nodded.

"And you're traveling alone?"

She nodded again, feeling a prickling sensation at the back of her neck. It happened whenever she became anxious, and right now she was very apprehensive about being questioned about her personal life. If there was anything she was highly sensitive about, it was either about work or *that*.

"That's very adventurous of you. Well, since you were so kind to help me today, Chanelle, I'm sure Vance here will be happy to help you in any way during the cruise. Right, son?"

Chanelle groaned inwardly. She was afraid to look at Vance. He must be feeling even more cornered than *her*.

"It would be…my pleasure," he drawled. He grinned as Adrien took a huge bite of a butter tart. "Would you care to join me for dinner, Chanelle? My family started without me, as I was at a meeting. They'll be leaving shortly and I'll be all by myself." His eyes glinted at her expectantly.

Chanelle's heart flipped. "Oh…um…sure," she said and, nodding to the group, she strode toward the nearest buffet, her nerve endings tingling knowing that Vance was right behind her.

When they returned to the table, Vance's family was ready to leave. "Goodbye, Chanelle," Betty said. "We'll be heading to Deck Five for the captain's event. Perhaps we'll see you there?"

"Perhaps." Chanelle didn't want to commit; *this* encounter had already made her feel somewhat overwhelmed. She smiled her goodbyes and tried to focus on enjoying the famous scallops from off the Nova Scotia coast while Vance dug into his *tourtière* and poutine. She glanced at him as he was licking a dribble of the cheesy gravy before it slid down to his chin, and the split second that he caught her gaze, she felt her insides quiver. He ran his tongue over his lips and then flashed her a grin. *"Je m'excuse,"* he apologized. "I adore Quebecois cuisine, and it adores my face." He slid his empty plate away and reached for the dessert plate. "And now for the pièce de résistance…"

* * *

Vance bit into his butter tart. It was sweet, but not as sweet as the woman sitting across from him, munching delicately on the lacy cookie she had chosen. Her auburn hair was gleaming in the sun that streamed through the window, and with the stunning dress she had chosen, she could easily be the subject of a painting.

Vance was convinced now that fate was deliberately making them cross paths.

It was impossible not to notice someone as beautiful as Chanelle. But being with her again, something deep inside him was telling him it was more than just her looks that was drawing his attention. It was her actions, whether it was the way she had sprung up for Adrien or how she had readily helped his mother.

He was seeing glimpses of her highly sensitive qualities, he realized. And he liked them just as much as her physical qualities…

They hadn't exchanged much conversation over dinner. She had seemed very pensive, and he hadn't wanted to disrupt her thoughts. As he bit into his second butter tart, a drop of syrup began to slide down one corner of his mouth. He saw Chanelle's mouth twitch and he laughed. "I told you, French Canadian food and I have this mutual attraction..."

Vance wiped his mouth with a napkin. Chanelle was gazing at him enigmatically, and he felt something shift inside his chest. He wanted to reach out and squeeze her hands and impulsively tell her that sharing her company had been another treat for him, and that he had also enjoyed their time together in the Sky Promenade and afterward at the fruit bar.

It was crazy, but despite his intention earlier to not seek her out, Vance suddenly wished he could take hold of Chanelle's hands and get her out of that chair and into his arms. Right or wrong, he wanted to taste her lips, and trail kisses down her neck to that lovely spot at the base of her neck where her pulse was softly beating.

His eyes burned with longing as he held her gaze, and a flicker in Chanelle's green hazel depths made him wonder if *she* could possibly be feeling the same way...

CHAPTER ELEVEN

CHANELLE DIDN'T KNOW if she should feel relieved or upset at the sudden appearance of a waiter with a jug of water to refill their glasses. For a moment there had been something in Vance's expression that had made her want to catch her breath. But when she transferred her gaze from the waiter back to Vance, whatever she had seen—or imagined—was gone.

He rose and asked her if she would be going to the captain's event. Unsure if he was leading up to asking her to accompany him, or if he was just being polite, Chanelle hesitated. Maybe that look in his eyes had just been a figment of her imagination. Like a mirage for a desert traveler seeking water…

So what had she been seeking? An indication that Vance Kingston—a seasoned playboy—had feelings for her? Feelings that went beyond a physical attraction?

You're delusional, her inner voice mocked.

Do you actually think this Zodiac magnate would be interested in you in that way? Wake up and smell the sea air, honey.

She saw Vance glance at his watch.

He was obviously anxious to get back to his family.

She stood up. "I think I'll just go back to my stateroom," she told him. "I've developed a bit of a headache, and if I rest awhile, it may not develop into a migraine."

Vance frowned. "Do you suffer from migraines often?"

"When I've been under a lot of stress, or if when the barometric pressure changes. Usually before my head starts pounding, I get a warning, an aura."

He raised his eyebrows. "What do you mean?"

"Auras can vary. For me, it's a zigzag that flashes in my eye, making it hard to focus," she said. "So if I'm looking at you, I don't see you the way you are. I see you like a Picasso painting…"

"Wow, I had no idea," he said. He peered at her closely, as he were expecting to see an aura develop right then and there. "Will you be okay to go back to your stateroom alone?"

"My vision is fine at the moment," Chanelle said drily. "Your features are perfectly in place."

And perfect, she added silently.

"If you *do* end up with a migraine, please don't hesitate to dial the medical facility. And if you want to de-stress, you might want to consider a spa treatment while you're here."

"Thanks. I'd better go. I'm keeping you from the captain's event," she said lightly.

"Not at all," he murmured. "Take care of yourself, Chanelle. And if you *do* feel better, I hope you consider coming back to the event."

She nodded and started to walk away. Of course she would take care of herself. But she had no intention of going to the captain's event with Vance. Even though she had seen something in his eyes moments earlier that had ignited a spark of excitement in her veins...

No, she tried to convince herself as she entered her stateroom and plopped down on the edge of her bed, she had only imagined something in Vance's eyes.

Chanelle caught sight of herself in mirrored panels on either side of the television unit. Her cheeks didn't need blush; they never had. They were quite rosy right now, a telltale sign of the anxiety caused by her ambivalent inner voices: *Vance Kingston is interested in you. There is no way Vance Kingston is interested in you.*

Chanelle couldn't imagine finding someone who would understand her sensitivities and the demands of her work. Her previous relationship had crumbled because she had made her work a priority.

Maybe she just didn't know how to be in a balanced relationship.

She had things to work out about herself... her job...her future. So how could she possibly entertain even the remotest idea of being with another man? It hadn't even crossed her mind when she had booked this cruise...

Chanelle shook her head in frustration. Here she was, stuck and feeling restless in her room, while people were enjoying themselves at events all over the ship. She could be at the featured artist event or magic show, or at the '70s disco party, or maybe trying out her luck at the casino...

Who was she kidding?

She probably didn't have the concentration

to sit through a gallery presentation, she didn't know if her head could take the blaring disco music and she didn't even gamble. Chanelle sighed and impatiently grabbed the pamphlet showing the evening's events. This was apparently the other side of Sagittarians. The negative side. Restless and impatient. Yup, that was *her* right now.

Chanelle tossed the pamphlet down. Being highly sensitive hadn't always worked in her favor over the years. She had taken herself out of play in many situations—often social ones in high school and university, and later, with work colleagues—because of her HSP sensibilities. Which meant she had missed out on fun opportunities because of her inhibitions and inability to loosen up. She hadn't given herself the chance to explore new friendships, new possibilities.

And in worrying about the negative, she had missed out on the positive.

She was still doing that.

It was time for her to stop second-guessing herself and start taking chances.

Take a leap of faith.

Chanelle stood up and smoothed down her dress. She would not stay cloistered in her stateroom and miss out on the fun on the ship. She freshened up, took a pill for her headache and, after applying a new coat of lip gloss, she grabbed her purse and made her way toward Deck Five.

Her brain might be trying to convince her that Vance Kingston had absolutely nothing to do with her decision, but deep down she knew the opposite was true.

And she was willing to risk everything to discover how he really felt about her by looking into his eyes…

The captain had welcomed everybody on deck, introduced some of his crew, and was now engaged in the photo session with guests. He'd be at it for a while, Vance thought, eyeing the line. In the meantime, the jazz musicians had begun their repertoire, and couples were already moving toward the dance floor. His mother, Mariah and Adrien had said their good-nights. They would be getting up fairly early to board the tender for Coral Haven, and so would he, but he had told them that he wanted to stay behind for a bit to enjoy the music and relaxed atmosphere.

That had been a white lie. He was waiting to see if Chanelle would come back. His anticipation had caused a tensing of his stomach muscles as he directed regular glances toward all the possible entry points she could take to Deck Five. He had almost finished his brandy, and he'd have to make up his mind whether to order another.

Occasionally a couple or small group of women would come up to chat with him. Some of the women glanced at him with undisguised interest, and he satisfied them with a generous smile and a group selfie if they asked.

The dance floor was filling up. The deck had a patio atmosphere, with strings of multicolored suspended lights that provided a soft illumination under the starry night. And sensual music that made you want to slow dance for hours...

If you had the right woman in your arms.

A waiter came by, and Vance ordered another brandy before walking to the railing to look out at the shifting waves. He couldn't help thinking that taking a cruise by oneself could be difficult emotionally, especially when couples were dancing nearby, their arms clasped tightly around each other.

Vance felt a jab in his gut. For the first time in his life, he had a feeling that there was something—no, *someone*—missing in his life. Not that his life had been devoid of women before his father had died. Far from it. But they had all been superficial relationships, with no commitment. He had never *pretended* to be committed. Wasn't that the reason he had earned the title of playboy? And he had enjoyed it for quite a while.

But those relationships were over. He didn't want superficial any longer, he realized. And as Vance stared at the expanse of sea under the stars, he realized something else: he needed to let go of the coping mechanisms he had subconsciously constructed in the past that had affected his relationships.

If he wanted more than just a temporary fling with a woman, he'd have to break down the walls of distrust around his heart and allow himself to be vulnerable. To not withhold his emotions in order to prevent himself from getting abandoned.

And hurt. Like he had done with his father.

His dad was gone.

And after his death, Vance had risked everything for the business. Yes, he had done it initially out of guilt, but as the weeks went by, the sense of guilt had diminished as his interest and passion for the company had grown.

And now his gut was telling him that he needed to take a new risk and allow himself to be open to a serious relationship...

He gulped back the remainder of his brandy. Turning around, his pulse spiked at the sight of Chanelle making her way past a group of couples who were chatting with drinks in hand. Vance saw every movement she made as if his vision had clicked to slow motion mode: the toss of her shiny auburn hair, the tentative smile on her poppy-red lips, the gentle sway of her hips in that fabulous dress and the even more fabulous curves of her legs. And how could he fail to notice the glances directed her way, both male and female?

Chanelle looked more enchanting than ever.

And Vance was more than ready to be enchanted. With his heart drumming so loud he couldn't hear the music around him, he headed toward her.

CHAPTER TWELVE

AT CHANELLE'S FIRST SCAN of the guests on deck, she didn't see Vance, and disappointment hit her like a cold wave. And then she spotted him leaving his place at the railing and walking toward her, and that cold wave turned into warm and bubbly surf.

Vance extended his hand and she took it, letting him lead her to a table for two further away from the musicians. He asked how she was feeling, and Chanelle told him that she was feeling better. She accepted his offer of a drink, and a waiter returned with a virgin Caesar for her and a coffee for Vance.

"I had my drinks before you arrived," he told her. "While I was sticking around to see if you'd come back." He looked at her with those intense blue eyes, and the warm feeling inside her climbed up a few notches.

They sat companionably as they listened to the music and watched the guests dancing.

When the jazz musicians took a break, two new performers proceeded to the stage with their Latin guitars. And when they began their second song, Vance asked her to dance.

She could hardly believe that here she was on the second night of the cruise, in the arms of Vance Kingston. *Slow dancing...*

Chanelle couldn't blame the drink for feeling as if she were up in the clouds, floating toward heaven. So the only thing she could blame was Vance Kingston, and his touch that was making her pulse throb erratically. And his spicy cologne that was driving her to distraction. She caught her breath as he pressed her closer, and her forehead brushed against his jawline. If she turned to the right, his lips would be close enough to...

This was madness. How had this happened?

Chanelle had not envisioned a man in the picture—*her picture*—for a long time. And a known playboy, who was doing what he did best: flirting and making her fall for him like every other woman he had played with in the past. Only, unlike those women, Chanelle was neither glamorous nor wealthy...

Chanelle stiffened as the stark truth hit her.

The stars in her eyes dissipated and left a dark, black void full of doubts.

"Are you okay, Chanelle?" Vance said huskily against her ear, and she realized that she had stopped dancing.

How could she possibly respond?

She didn't want to be rude, but she had to protect herself. These were dangerous waters she had entered. And judging from her body's reaction to the man who had led her there, she had to make her way back to safe shores before something happened that she would regret. In a few days, the cruise would be over. She was delusional if she thought this shipboard flirting could lead to anything else. She had to put a stop to it.

Now. She was way out of her league.

"My headache's back," she lied. "I think I'll just return to my stateroom."

Vance's blue eyes pierced hers. He didn't release her hand, nor his arm around her waist.

"We can go somewhere quieter..."

"I don't think—" Chanelle hesitated as a couple, locked in an embrace, bumped into them.

Chanelle and Vance broke apart, and after

the couple apologized and continued dancing, Vance said brusquely, "Okay, let's go."

Chanelle felt his arm around her as he ushered her inside and she was conscious of a few curious gazes following them. Were they thinking that she and Vance…? Her cheeks burned. She hadn't expected Vance to accompany her.

When they got to her stateroom, Chanelle unlocked the door, opened it a crack, then turned to Vance. "Good night," she murmured.

His eyes glittered down at her. "How can it be, when you don't trust me?"

Chanelle's eyes widened. She opened her mouth and then shut it, completely at a loss for words.

"Chanelle, I haven't known you for very long, but from the time I *have* spent with you, I have picked up on a few cues. Like how your lovely cheeks flame up when you're feeling stressed or distressed." He cocked his head at her appraisingly. "Now I could be wrong, but I have a wild hunch that you were worried about my intentions and therefore had to come up with an excuse to leave."

Chanelle's cheeks were burning. She heard voices approaching from the end of the hall and quickly opened the door wider. The last thing she wanted was people seeing who was at her stateroom door at this time of night. "Please come in for a minute," she urged.

A few moments later, she had no choice but to face him. And be truthful.

She sighed. "I'm sorry I had to make up a fib this time. I was telling the truth earlier, though, and I did take a pill before going to Deck Five." She looked up at him warily.

Vance's mouth quirked, and he reached over to take one of her hands. "Chanelle, I'm not your confessor," he said huskily. "But please tell me if I'm right. I can handle it." His eyes met hers without wavering.

Chanelle bit her lip. He had spoken candidly and hadn't sounded as if he were playing games with her or trying to manipulate her in any way. "You're right," she conceded. "I don't know you very well, and I'm not sure I can trust your intentions. And if you want me to be honest—" she eyed him defensively "—your reputation precedes you."

Vance's eyes narrowed. "Ouch. But thanks for being honest." He looked down at her hand in his and was silent for a few moments. When he looked up, there was regret in the depths of his eyes.

Chanelle felt a twinge of guilt. She hadn't intended to hurt his feelings. *So now what?*

"The past is the past," he said quietly. "I can't undo that, Chanelle. But I'm not the same man I was nine months ago, and the years before that." He gently let go of her hand. "The death of a family member changes you…"

Chanelle felt a lump in her throat as Vance's voice wavered. Maybe it had been wrong of her to bring up his reputation, but it had slipped out before she could think clearly.

She realized the stateroom was dark except for the dim light in the entrance. She should turn on the other lights.

"Now that I know how *you* feel, Chanelle, would you want to hear the truth about *my* feelings?"

"You must feel that I'm judging you…"

"No worries. I have a thick skin. Or rather, a layer of chain mail under these clothes." He suddenly grinned at her. "I'm not called Sir Vancelot for nothing."

Chanelle couldn't help smiling, and some of the tension in the air seemed to dissipate.

"So may I have your ear, Lady Chanelle?"

"I suppose I can spare a minute or two," she murmured. "But then you'll have to go. I've booked an early excursion tomorrow on Grand Cayman." She strode into the room and turned on a light. She sat on one edge of the couch and Vance sat down beside her.

"Swimming with the stingrays?"

"*Not!* With my sensitive skin, I'd probably break out in some kind of a rash."

"Going to Hell?"

"Pardon?"

Vance chuckled. "It's a town named for its unique rock formations. It's part of the island tour and includes the turtle center."

Chanelle laughed. "For a moment I was about to tell *you* where to go!"

Vance burst out laughing. "And I called you a *lady*?"

Chanelle pretended to look at him with disdain.

"Well, where will you be heading, my lady?"

Chanelle felt something flip in her chest at the smile in his voice and eyes as he said *my lady*. "I'm heading to a beach with the name of some kind of alcohol. Whisky Beach or something to that effect."

He chuckled again. "Rum Point Beach."

"Yes, that's it! Rum, whisky—it's all the same to me, since I indulge in neither."

"You're a funny lady."

"Why? Because I don't drink much?" Chanelle frowned at him, confused.

"Because you make me laugh."

"Is that what you wanted to tell me? That you find me amusing?"

Vance gazed at her without responding for a few moments. And then he placed his hand over hers. An inner voice told her to move her hand away, but a stronger voice said the opposite. She couldn't tear her gaze away, either.

"I want to tell you a lot of things, Chanelle. Yes, I find you amusing. And kind. And dedicated. And—" he squeezed her hand gently "—and beautiful." His eyes seemed to darken as they gazed into hers with such intensity that she caught her breath. And then he was leaning toward her, and the magnetic force that his eyes had ignited seemed to be pulling her toward him as well.

When their lips touched, her eyes closed au-

tomatically and she was unable to process anything else but the instinctive need to respond.
She felt Vance release her hand, and a moment
later both his hands were cupping her face,
deepening his kiss until her whole body tin-
gled. Had a kiss ever felt this sweet? This...
delicious?

When he finally pulled back gently to look
into her eyes again, Chanelle felt like she was
swimming in their darkest, deepest, most plea-
surable depths.

She traced her fingers against the stubble of
his jaw. Vance caught his breath and suddenly
brought her hand down. "I need to go now,
Chanelle," he said gruffly. "I'm sorry, but I
don't want to stay and have you regret it later."

Vance felt like an absolute heel, leaving
Chanelle with that look in her eyes. The look
of a dejected puppy. But how could he stay
without knowing for sure that she wasn't just
caught up in the moment and later wouldn't
blame him for taking advantage of her?

Kissing her had been his first big mistake.
Yes, she had responded, and yes, he had wanted
to continue, but something inside him had

tugged on the reins of his passion and made him stop. Chanelle Robinson was vulnerable. She had had two big changes in her life in the past year and had booked this cruise to relax and make choices about her future, not get involved with *him*.

Vance returned to his stateroom and walked out to his balcony. He watched the waves rising and cresting, and he felt a similar agitation inside. A swell of happiness that Chanelle was attracted to him, and then a sense of deflation that somehow he had handled it all wrong.

He should have kept it light. They had been laughing, caught up in a play of words, and he had to go and spoil it by letting his testosterone take over.

Vance groaned. He could have even stopped after he had told her that she was beautiful. But he hadn't been content with the sparkle that had lit up her eyes at his words. He had wanted further proof of her feelings…

Well, he had gotten proof, all right. But when Chanelle had demonstrated her desire, his inner voice had abruptly broken through the sweetness of her kiss to tell him to slow things down, that she was vulnerable and that she needed space to work things out in her life.

He started to unbutton his shirt when a tentative knock on his door made him freeze. His heart jangled against his rib cage. He leaped to open it, but it wasn't Chanelle standing there. He tried to control his emotions and smiled at the environmental director he had met with earlier. He and Pauline had become friends since he had started working at Zodiac, and she would be leaving the next morning for her upcoming wedding on Grand Cayman Island at the end of the week.

She handed him a gift box. "Since I won't be at the gala to celebrate your new position, *President Kingston*," she said, hugging him.

"Thanks, Pauline. And I have a surprise for you when we're all back in Toronto."

"Sounds good," she said with a laugh. "I like surprises."

He wished her the best, gave her another hug and watched her leave. Turning to reenter his stateroom, he started at the sight of Chanelle halfway down the opposite hallway, her face as frozen as her body. She had intended to come to his stateroom, he realized, only to find him hugging another woman who was just leaving.

He had to explain…

But before her name had finished leaving his lips, Chanelle had turned around swiftly and disappeared around the corner.

CHAPTER THIRTEEN

AFTER VANCE HAD left her stateroom, Chanelle had remained transfixed on the couch, her face feeling as numb as her brain. What had just happened?

Vance had ignited something within her that she had never experienced in her previous relationship. A combination of feelings that had produced an alchemy that was powerful, magical.

A desire to know Vance to the core.

The magic had been sparked by his touch, his kiss, his words...

And then he had pulled away.

Because he had thought that if he stayed, she might regret it later...

He couldn't have been more wrong.

Chanelle had stared woodenly at the door, considering a swirl of other possible reasons for his decision. Farfetched though it seemed, could it be that deep down, he was worried about her motives?

That she was really after his money and was trying to ensnare him?

Chanelle did not want to accept the excuse Vance had used. He had pinned his decision on *her*, making it look as if he was considering her feelings before his own. Feelings that she *might* have regrets if they had allowed their passion to play out...but then, she *was* terrified of getting hurt again. Did she go into self-protection mode whenever things got serious? Maybe...

But *he* had decided to play it safe and deny them both what they had been close—*so close*—to experiencing.

And he hadn't given her a say about it.

Chanelle had felt shortchanged. With an unexpected surge of warrior determination, she had leaped off the couch and decided to talk to Vance, thinking that at the very least, she could ask him to open up about his true feelings, just as she intended to be about *hers*.

And then, whatever would be, would be...

Minutes later, the elevator had opened to the lobby on Vance's deck. Chanelle's nerve endings were practically crackling, and she had breathed deeply to try to steady her heartbeat. She had turned into the long hallway, only to spot a woman wearing the familiar Zodiac employee blazer hugging Vance. And then he was telling the woman that he had a surprise for her when they were back in Toronto. She had laughed, and then Vance had given her another hug.

At this point Chanelle's feet had felt cemented to the floor. Like in a nightmare, with her vocal cords frozen as well.

Seconds later, Vance had gazed *her* way, and Chanelle had clearly seen the dismay on his face.

She hadn't wanted to stick around. Nothing he attempted to say would have mended the gash in her heart.

Once a playboy, always a playboy, she had thought bitterly as her gaze dropped to his unbuttoned shirt. And she had turned and fled, taking the stairs instead of waiting for the elevator. It was only when she had arrived back in her stateroom, and she had bolted the door, that she had burst into tears.

Damn him, she thought now between sobs. He had played her for a fool. No wonder he hadn't wanted to stay. He had planned an *encounter* with an employee he was obviously involved with on the ship and back in Toronto.

Well, he could have her. And while he was at it, he could also go to hell.

Vance had considered running after Chanelle but had decided against it. She would not have wanted a scene of any kind in front of other guests. He would wait awhile and then go and knock on her stateroom door. And hope that she would let him in and give him the chance to explain.

Would she hear him out after what she had witnessed? Being highly sensitive, Chanelle would have arrived at the worst possible conclusion about him. And he couldn't blame her.

Putting himself in her shoes, he could understand why she wouldn't want to face him. She had been on her way to see him—that alone made his heart twinge—only to find him hugging another woman. And Chanelle must have heard the exchange between him and Pauline as well. His promise of a surprise when they were back in Toronto…

He had to talk to Chanelle. Make her understand...

Vance had another thought. Chanelle was probably not only thinking the worst about *him*, but also about herself. That hurt even more. He groaned. Chanelle had had a rough year personally and professionally, and the tenuous feelings of trust that she had shown him must have immediately shattered. He had seen it on her face.

She would be blaming herself for having allowed him to get so close...and feeling humiliated...

Vance rose and strode to the door. It was almost midnight, but there would be no rest tonight unless he got through to Chanelle. He did up the buttons on his shirt and headed to her stateroom, his pulse as fast as his footsteps.

CHAPTER FOURTEEN

CHANELLE LOOKED AT herself in the bathroom mirror. Her eye makeup had smeared from all the crying she had done, and her eyelids were puffy. *Absolutely beautiful*, she thought bitterly, using Vance's earlier words.

Chanelle was too upset to even attempt sleeping, so instead of changing into her teddy, she put on a pair of shorts and a T-shirt. Knowing that her thoughts would just continue to torment her, she turned on the TV and started flicking the channels mindlessly. Propped up on pillows against the headboard, she felt a flutter of anxiety at the thought of having to spend three more days on the cruise with the possibility of crossing paths with Vance.

If she did run into him, she would not let him see how shattered she was. She had her pride.

And she had absolutely no intention of seeking him out. *Not a chance in hell*. She had allowed herself to succumb to his charms and had ended up feeling like a complete fool.

As she continued changing the channels, Chanelle realized she was clenching her jaw again. And watching TV wasn't helping. She pressed the off switch and turned off all the lights except the lamp by her bedside. She breathed in deeply and tried to focus on the sound of the waves from the open balcony door.

Her attempt at mindful meditation was interrupted by a soft tap at her door. Chanelle felt her stomach coil instantly into a hard knot. She remained motionless. Had it been her imagination?

The knock came again. "Chanelle? Please give me a chance to explain…"

Chanelle's heart tumbled crazily against her rib cage. She couldn't believe that Vance had the nerve to think that she would give him the time of day. Or night. The last thing she intended on doing was opening the door and letting him in. She had made that mistake once, and she wouldn't be so foolish as to allow him in her space again.

"Chanelle? I know it sounds like a cliché,

but it's not what you think. You'll understand if you let me in."

Vance was keeping his voice low, but Chanelle could hear both urgency and frustration in it.

"I don't want to explain out in the hall... Please answer, Chanelle."

Chanelle turned off her lamp and pulled the covers over her head.

There's your answer, Mr. Kingston.

She woke up to a baby-blue sky that was painted with soft brushes of pink. It was such a peaceful sight and a sharp contrast to how she felt inside. She couldn't get the memory of Vance and the woman out of her mind. She had had a troubled sleep, waking up every two to three hours, and at one point, she had almost been tempted to go to an upper deck to walk around and clear her head.

Chanelle was glad she had set her cell phone alarm. She couldn't wait to get off the ship and spend the day by herself on Rum Point Beach. Sure, there would be other guests who would be thinking along the same lines, but she was determined to find a quiet spot and just forget everything that had happened to her so far.

She stepped into the shower and tried to keep thoughts of Vance from following her in. *Fat chance.* How could she forget the feel of him as they danced? The muscled shoulders, his hand firmly clasping hers…and then later, the heady sensation as his lips took possession of hers…

Stop! He used you!

Chanelle turned off the shower. *That's* what she should be focusing on, not his body or his lips, she thought, scowling. She wrapped herself in the guest bathrobe and a few moments later changed into a navy bikini before slipping on a knee-length yellow cotton dress with eyelet accents and spaghetti straps. The multicolored wrap bracelet Kayla had given her was her only accessory.

Chanelle prepared a large beach bag with the essentials and then checked the time. Room service should be arriving shortly. Another smart decision she had made yesterday. She would have her coffee and toast and then make her way down to the tender station on Deck Two. She would at least enjoy the beach today, Chanelle promised herself. And there would be nothing or nobody to prevent that from happening.

Least of all Vance Kingston.

Chanelle took the elevator down to Deck Two. She had received a call from Guest Services while she was having her coffee, advising her that her time to board the tender had changed. For unspecified reasons, she would be leaving half an hour later than she had planned.

When she arrived, there was a group just about to get onboard. She rushed to join them and presented her identification card to one of the security officials. A whistle sounded, and a few moments later, the group proceeded to board. There was a substantial breeze, so Chanelle opted for the covered lower deck. She made her way carefully down the steps, glad to see there were plenty of good seats.

She made her way toward the back, and a sudden shuffling made her look to her right. Her heart felt like it was about to rocket out of her chest...

Chanelle swayed sharply as the tender started moving, and she plopped down hard on the seat closest to her, just arm's length away from where Vance Kingston was standing. And at the far end of the tender, his family was smiling and waving at her.

Vance wished Chanelle would have heard him out last night. He had stared at the door of her stateroom for a few minutes after his last appeal, hoping that Chanelle would change her mind. He had gotten the message loud and clear when he saw from the space at the bottom of the door that she had turned off the light. Giving up, he had headed back to his own stateroom.

He had felt like a total jerk to have hurt Chanelle, even if it *had* been unintentional. And none of it would have happened if he had just continued kissing her instead of leaving her at such a vulnerable moment.

But where would they be now if he had let himself give in to the passion that had been steadily building inside him?

He had to make amends to Chanelle.

For several hours, Vance had racked his brain as to how he should handle this highly sensitive situation with an even more highly sensitive person. Staring up at the ceiling above his bed,

Vance had come up with a few ideas and then scrapped them. And then he remembered that she was heading to Rum Point Beach. And he and his family would be taking one of the tenders to Coral Haven. The passengers would all be getting off at Grand Cayman, and Vance's tender would continue on.

The only thing he had to do was to ensure Chanelle boarded the same tender he would already be on. That could be arranged with a quick call. And then Vance would attempt to make another appeal for Chanelle to hear him out. And if he couldn't convince her, she'd still have the option of getting off at Grand Cayman. If Chanelle continued to Coral Haven, it would have to be entirely of her own free will.

Vance met Chanelle's incredulous stare with a polite nod. He had known that it would be as awkward as hell trying to discuss the matter between them with people all around, but he had no other option. He would give it his best shot, and if Chanelle could be convinced to remain onboard instead of going with her original plan, they would be heading to a place that Vance considered heaven on earth. While Mariah, Adrien and his mother relaxed in one section of the rambling villa his father had had built five years ago, Vance would have a better opportunity to set things right with Chanelle.

And if the stars and planets were all aligned in his favor, he and Chanelle would spend an idyllic day together before the tender arrived to take them back to the *Aquarius*.

Vance closed the distance between them by sitting opposite her. He leaned forward. "Chanelle, I can't say a lot now, but I promise you'll understand if you let me explain."

Chanelle's cheeks were like smoldering coals, but her eyes flashed ice. "Oh, I understand," she said stiffly, keeping her voice low.

She turned her gaze away from him to look out at the scenery. He felt bad that her first excursion off the ship had to be tainted by bad feelings. If only she would gaze into his eyes and see the genuine tenderness he felt for her. But of course she couldn't, with the thorn-covered glasses she was wearing...

Vance gazed at Chanelle's profile and felt his heart expanding. It wasn't just *tenderness* he felt for her, for God's sake, it was more than that. It was a truly happy feeling that had eluded him in the past, even when he had thought he was enjoying himself with other women. It was the feeling that he had found a rare treasure when those green-hazel eyes had sparkled under the patio lights on Deck Five.

It was the way his heart had vaulted when she returned his kiss...

Maybe he wasn't quite ready to put a name to it just yet, but if it was what he thought it was, he'd find the right way to let Chanelle know...

Before time ran out on him.

CHAPTER FIFTEEN

COULD *ANY* MAN be trusted? Chanelle tried to focus on the enchanting views of palm trees and charming villas as the tender sped past, but Vance's proximity made it impossible. The lump of bitterness and disillusionment that had settled in her throat and stomach after last night's discovery hadn't lessened any, and now, facing Vance but unable to express herself with so many people around them, Chanelle felt frustrated. And angry.

Chanelle swayed forward as the tender hit a choppy patch of water, and she caught her breath as Vance's arms shot out to steady her. His face was inches away from hers, and now she could see the faded blue of his eyes and the shadows beneath. His Adam's apple bobbed as he swallowed.

He hadn't slept much, either, she thought. Could it have been the result of a guilty conscience? *Good.*

As Chanelle stared at him defiantly, something in Vance's expression made her falter.

There was something there that was different than the way he had looked at her in the past. A look of...of *sadness* that seemed to reach across and connect with something in her own eyes.

And then he smiled at her as he released his hold, but the sadness remained in his eyes.

Chanelle felt a vague urge to let him explain. Her heart started drumming.

Should she relent and at least hear him out?

A chorus of excited voices distracted her. A group of passengers around her rushed off to get a better view of something in the waters.

"A pod of porpoises," Vance said. "Always a delight for tourists."

Chanelle started to rise, but she hesitated as Vance touched her arm. "Can we talk? At least while this diversion lasts?"

Chanelle looked down at his hand at the same time that he withdrew it. His touch, although gentle, had sent a sizzle along her nerve endings. She felt a flush creep up her neck. Taking a deep breath, she sat back down.

He was leaning forward, his brow creased above blue eyes that startled her with their clarity. "Chanelle, I know you're planning to go to Rum Point Beach. But I don't think you'll be able to enjoy it fully with this misunderstanding between us. If you give me a chance, I will clear everything up."

Chanelle raised her eyebrows. How much could he clear up with her before the passengers returned to their seats? "This—this is awkward," she admitted. "I should never have—"

"No, Chanelle. I take full responsibility. I want to explain—better than I did last night—why I needed to leave. And that the person you saw at my door is not who you think she is."

They both turned at another wave of excited shouts from the passengers.

"Look, Chanelle." His voice had a sudden note of urgency. "In a minute—or less—they'll be back and we won't be able to talk. I need more time. I'm asking you to trust me and to stay on the tender. Come to Coral Haven with me instead of going to Rum Point Beach. There will be time and space to make things right." His eyes bored into her like blue spears. "I want to make things right with you, Chanelle."

The passengers started clapping. "That's the

end of the porpoise show," Vance said. "And we're almost at Grand Cayman…"

Chanelle had no time to respond as the passengers made their way noisily back to their seats. Her eyes met Vance's as a couple of teenagers zipped past them. No, there was no time—or space—to hear him out.

Do you want to?

She bit her lip, the thrumming in her chest increasing as the tender neared the shore. Moments later, the passengers started to file up the stairway and out, and Chanelle knew she had less than a minute to make a decision. She glanced at Vance's mother and sister, who were absorbed in something Adrien was saying.

Chanelle glanced quickly at the family now exiting the tender. She stood up, her knees feeling wobbly. If she was going to leave, she'd have to go. Now.

Her gaze flew to Vance. He hadn't moved, but his eyes were fixed on hers like lasers. Her brain willed her body to start walking, but her feet were rooted to the floor of the tender.

Chanelle opened her mouth to say something, but the whistle of the tender operator startled her. She bit her lip and, feeling a tremor of anticipation course through her, she promptly sat down.

Vance's heart had jolted when Chanelle had stood up, but when, timeless seconds later, she sat down, his heart had started pumping so hard that he almost put his hand over it to try to calm it down.

This was big. He had seen the indecision on Chanelle's face, the flicker of a frown as she debated in those few seconds whether she should leave and proceed to her excursion on Rum Point Beach or stay and give him the chance to explain. He was both stunned and elated at Chanelle's decision.

He wanted to say something, but his words were stuck in his throat. Chanelle had turned slightly to look out at the activity on Grand Cayman, and he was relieved to have some time to process the impact of her decision. And his reaction to it.

Vance hadn't taken it for granted that she would choose to continue on to Coral Haven. And he had felt a current of indecision himself before he suggested it to her. Was he doing the right thing? Why was he choosing to make things right with a woman he had known for less than two days? And why was he bringing her to Coral Haven? He hadn't brought Brianna there, despite her not-so-subtle hints that she'd love to see his island.

He knew he was complicating things. He had sacrificed so much of the last nine months to the promise he had made to lead the company. He had made it his top priority. Nothing had competed with his razor-sharp intentions. Nothing and nobody. Especially a woman. He had instinctively known that to succeed, he had to suspend his playboy inclinations. At least until he had proven himself at Zodiac Cruises.

But something had changed since he had stepped onboard the *Aquarius*. In his previous relationships, Vance had played it safe, controlling the extent of his emotions. He hadn't allowed himself to become emotionally entangled with any woman. And they had seemed satisfied—for the most part—with the limited scope of his intentions.

It was different with Chanelle. No other woman in the past had intrigued him the way she had. Instantly. And after two days of spending time with her, something deep inside was telling him he needed to take a risk with this woman. Risk showing her that he genuinely cared about her feelings. About her.

He wanted more with her.

And he had to find out if there was any chance that she wanted more with him. If she would let him teach her how to trust.

He couldn't play it safe anymore, and he couldn't toy with Chanelle's emotions. The only way to discover what she wanted was to act now, before the cruise ended and she went back home.

Which was why he had had to provide an opportunity for them to be together.

He wanted more than just work in his life. He didn't want to end up like his father. And he knew now that he wanted—needed—more than just a physical relationship.

He wanted love.

Vance gazed at Chanelle's profile. He felt an ache in his chest, but it wasn't painful. It was an ache of longing, of anticipation, knowing he had to make a conscious decision to take a risk. A risk at letting love in.

He watched the breeze ruffling the long, thick waves of Chanelle's hair. Her complexion was peach soft, with a rosy glow on her cheekbones. He caught a whiff of her perfume, its sweet peach scent making him feel like he was in an orchard in BC's Okanagan Valley or in Ontario's Niagara-on-the-Lake. He breathed in deeply, and at that moment, she tossed her hair back and met his gaze.

She blinked at him wordlessly, the sweeping motion of her eyelashes over green-hazel eyes mesmerizing him, the curve and fullness of her lips making his pulse quicken. He wanted to talk to her, but they were a few minutes away from Coral Haven, and he didn't want to start something he couldn't finish.

He would get that chance soon enough…

CHAPTER SIXTEEN

CHANELLE HEARD ADRIEN shout something excitedly. She pulled her gaze away from Vance's and saw that they were approaching an island. Coral Haven. She drew in a breath, already enchanted by what she saw. The surf cresting on the whitest beach she had ever seen, leaving what looked like the scallop-edged lace hem of a wedding gown. Lush vegetation and palm trees swaying in the breeze. And glimpses of a sprawling villa beyond with its coral facade, canopied windows and elegant balconies.

"Pinch me," she murmured, and then realized she had said it aloud.

"I would," Vance replied huskily. "But I'd get into trouble with my mother."

How was she supposed to respond to that?

Fortunately, she didn't have to. Vance answered his cell phone, and Chanelle couldn't help hearing his responses to someone called Valentina, thanking her and Carlos for looking after the villa and preparing it for their visit. He told Valentina the tender was approaching and just minutes away, and her response made him chuckle. "I'm sure 'the little breakfast' you prepared for us is more like a banquet, Valentina." He glanced over at Chanelle. "So it's a good thing I've brought an extra guest."

Another pause followed by a deep laugh. "No, Valentina, the only Mrs. Kingston with me is my mother. My *other* mother besides *you*," he joked.

Moments later, the tender was moored near a large boathouse and Chanelle waited for Vance's mother, sister and nephew to precede her as they stepped onto the long dock. Vance followed behind her, and as the rest of his family strode briskly toward the path that would lead to the villa, Chanelle slowed her pace to gaze around her. The view was stunning, with the clear azure water lapping at the pristine shore, changing to various hues of turquoise in deeper waters.

"Do you still want me to pinch you?" Vance's amused voice behind her made Chanelle realize that she had stopped walking altogether.

"Thanks, but no thanks," she returned with

a slight edge. "I can usually bring myself back to reality without having to be pinched." She quickened her pace.

"Chanelle, you know I'd never hurt you." His voice was soft as he stepped up beside her.

"Well, you have," she blurted, forgetting her earlier intention of not letting him see how shattered she was. She felt a prickle behind her eyelids but couldn't bring herself to look at him.

"Uncle Vance!" Adrien left his mother's side to run back toward them. "Can you come and swing with me in the gazebo? Mommy's going inside to help Valentina, and Grandma's going to check on the rose garden..."

Vance bent to catch Adrien as he approached and lifted him high over his head. Adrien squealed, "Let me down, let me down," but as soon as Vance complied, he cried, "Lift me up, lift me up!"

Vance burst out laughing, and Chanelle couldn't help smiling. Their gazes met when Vance, holding a giggling Adrien up in the air, turned to glance at her. Despite her comment moments earlier, Chanelle felt a sizzle run through her at Vance's boyish grin. The rest of him was anything but boyish, she couldn't help thinking as he brought Adrien back down. Her gaze took in his strong shoulders and muscled biceps, enhanced by his tan T-shirt. His well-fitting jeans couldn't disguise his muscular legs, either.

The dock ended and a charming stone walkway began, flanked on both sides by agave and other exotic plant species that made Chanelle catch her breath with their vibrant colors. An artist's paradise, she thought, her gaze flitting from the brilliant multicolored crotons and hibiscus varieties to the giant pink-and-coral peony blooms that perfumed the air as they walked past. She caught her breath at the variety of orchids. She had read up on the flora of the islands and had learned that there were twenty-six varieties of native orchids, and one in particular called the wild banana orchid, which was the Cayman Islands' national flower.

Chanelle gasped when the sprawling two-story villa came into full view, with bougainvillea spilling over balconies and yellow-green canopies adding charm above the windows of the coral stucco walls. Absolutely enchanting.

Her gaze wandered to a courtyard featuring white rattan furniture with red-and-yellow floral cushions and giant glazed pots bursting with flowers of the same color. Four umbrella tables were set with cut flower arrangements in decorative clay vases, and two hammocks swayed slightly in the breeze at one edge of the courtyard, near the rose garden that Vance's mother was now inspecting.

"The pool and gazebo are on the other side of the villa," Vance told her, as Adrien pulled him in that direction. "Why don't you join us, Chanelle?"

They disappeared around a bend before Chanelle could reply. She gazed toward the beautiful rounded door of the villa. It was painted the same green as the window canopies and looked like an illustration from one of Chanelle's childhood fairy-tale collections.

Chanelle strode quickly toward the path Vance and Adrien had taken. Things might be strained between her and Vance, but she didn't really want to put herself in a position where she would be open to questioning by the women in Vance's family.

And at least Adrien would be a buffer. She

wasn't ready to be alone with Vance again. *Not just yet...*

The other side of the villa was just as breathtaking, with its wraparound porch and massive sunroom. The pool area, with its outside bar and elegant chaise lounges, was an oasis in itself, with potted palms and water fountains and an outdoor shower at each end. The center tiles at the bottom of the pool featured the Zodiac Cruises name and logo, and the twelve zodiac signs were displayed on the outer tiles.

Chanelle felt like she was in another world. Vance's lifestyle was so far removed from her own. Why, her entire apartment could fit in the sunroom. She sighed. It wasn't that she was begrudging any of the Kingstons their material possessions. Vance's parents had worked hard to achieve their success, making many sacrifices at the beginning, according to the online articles she had read about their rise to success in the cruise business. And now Vance was leading the company, showing initiative and a fierce commitment to its continuing success.

Chanelle watched the soon-to-be official president of Zodiac Cruises swinging away with his nephew in the gazebo, grinning as if he were a kid at the midway. It was a huge white structure on a solid foundation, with an overhanging roof and rolled-up canvas panels between its twelve wooden posts. On the end opposite the swing, there was a hammock big enough for two people, a bistro set and a bar-size refrigerator.

Chanelle couldn't help wondering if Vance had made use of the gazebo with any of his female friends on sultry island nights... All he'd have to do was to roll down the canvas panels and he'd have a summer bedroom...and a bottle of wine in the fridge waiting to be savored...

Vance's gaze met hers as she stood a few feet away from them, and he waved her over, bringing the swing to a stop. "Come and join us," he called. "There's nothing more relaxing than an old-fashioned ride on a swing."

Chanelle eyed the swing. She would sit across from Vance and Adrien. She could handle *that*.

But could she handle having those blue eyes continue to look at her that way?

Vance tried not to make it obvious, but he couldn't help gazing at Chanelle and the striking picture she made. No, *striking* wasn't the perfect word. She was eye candy in her yellow dress with its eyelet sections, revealing glimpses of navy and bare skin underneath. And her bare shoulders—under the thinnest spaghetti straps—and curvy legs elicited thoughts that made his heart drum an erratic beat against his ribs.

He couldn't believe that she was actually here on Coral Haven, especially after he had basically given her the brush-off last night. The excuse he had tried to convince himself with was that Chanelle might have regretted it later if he had stayed. And that had been a valid supposition, but there had also been another reason why he had backed off. *Fear.* Fear that making love to Chanelle would force him into a commitment, and he hadn't been sure that he had it in him to commit to a serious relationship.

He didn't exactly have a good track record when it came to commitment… But then again, he had never met a woman he had wanted to commit to.

He had screwed up with Chanelle. But now he had the opportunity to make things right. Explain his reasons. *His fears.* Show Chanelle that he wasn't playing with her emotions or with anyone else's.

As soon as he could get her alone…

Valentina had prepared a feast. The gleaming modern sideboard displayed platters of croissants, pastries, steaming omelets and sausages. She had put on the strong coffee that Vance and Mariah preferred and Earl Grey tea for their mother.

Minutes earlier, Valentina had sounded a bell, and after rolling down the canvas panels of the gazebo to keep it cool, he, Chanelle and Adrien had gone inside. Vance had introduced Chanelle, and Valentina had given Vance a wink and an approving nod before leaving for the day.

Breakfast was not as awkward as Vance thought it might be. Mariah was treating Chanelle like a longtime girlfriend. And his mother was chatting easily with Chanelle about her rose garden.

Vance reached for another custard-filled croissant. There was no rush to do anything but enjoy the moment. And he certainly was enjoying how things were playing out with Chanelle and his family.

It shouldn't be too long before he had Chanelle all to himself...

CHAPTER SEVENTEEN

AFTER VANCE'S MOTHER and sister had left to go up to their respective rooms, Vance turned to Chanelle. "Look," he said, "we're here for a good stretch. I *do* want to explain what happened last night…and apologize for any misunderstanding…but could you just indulge me for a few minutes and let me show you around the place?" He tilted his head at her—if she wasn't so upset with him, she'd find his puppy dog look humorous.

Chanelle pursed her lips. Maybe he was trying to ease into it…and maybe she needed a few moments to mentally prepare what to say to *him*. "Fine," she said coolly, wishing those baby-blue eyes weren't so easy to look at. She couldn't let them distract her from the reality of his true nature…even though he had made her feel things she never thought she would feel again…

Despite her intentions to remain indifferent,

Chanelle found herself captivated by the beautiful rooms and eclectic furnishings. She found herself listening as Vance explained how his mother's love of antiques was reflected in areas like the main floor living room, with its mahogany Chippendale highboy and gleaming secretary desk, along with more traditional floral upholstery.

His preference for elegant simplicity was the inspiration for the sunroom, he told her, indicating the ivory Italian leather couches and scarlet cushions positioned around a red-lacquered circular coffee table. Chanelle's eyes widened at the massive bay window that overlooked the pool and gazebo area and provided a stunning view of the beach a short distance away.

Vance had selected many of the paintings throughout the villa, and he gave Chanelle a blurb about each artist and the inspiration behind the work.

"Wow," she said. "I didn't expect you—"

"To be so smart?" His mouth twisted wryly, and he gazed down at her with raised eyebrows.

"That's not exactly what I meant," she said, flushing.

"I *did* major in art history and design, and before stepping into my father's shoes, I curated an art gallery. Although I sadly neglected my own art after discovering the art of being a playboy," he added wistfully.

Chanelle's eyes widened. How could he be so...so *casual* about it?

"Forgive me for being blunt, Chanelle, but it is what it is. My parents weren't very happy, as you can imagine. My mother wanted me to use my degree in some capacity in the company—designing and overseeing the art galleries and auctions, for example—but I was caught up in my own self-indulgent world. And I couldn't see myself working for or with my father."

"You didn't get along?" Chanelle ventured.

Vance gave a curt laugh. "Ah...*no*. He was barely around. He was a workaholic. And when he did come home, he made it clear that he had no use for my art."

Chanelle felt a pang at his words. She understood what being a workaholic was all about. And now she could see how that had affected her relationship.

"Both sides lose out," she murmured. "It must have been hard having a father but hardly ever seeing him. And having him not take your art seriously."

"I had a hard time investing any emotions—positive ones, that is—in an absentee father," he said, his voice steely. "And I swore I'd never turn out like him."

His gaze shifted to a stunning landscape on one of the walls of the sunroom. She had recognized it immediately as a painting by one of the iconic Group of Seven upon entering the room. Now at close range, she saw that it was one of J. E. H. MacDonald's scenic landscapes. Vance turned to Chanelle. "I like to have a bit of Canada with me when I'm away." He smiled. "I also have a Lawren Harris in my bedroom. I was inspired by the Group of Seven. I started sketching and painting in high school and had filled a sketchpad with my drawings to show that I was serious about pursuing art at university." His smile disappeared. "My father got angry. Tossed it aside. For him it was get involved in the company or nothing. And back then, I chose the nothing."

"Our past experiences and choices help make us who we are," Chanelle said. "When we're young, we subconsciously tell ourselves stories in order to cope with our situation. You internalized the fact that your father put his work before you and probably concluded that he didn't love you. But now, as an adult, having stepped into his shoes for the last nine months, your perspective has probably changed a little. Maybe you can see that he was focused on building a future for you, possibly because his father wasn't able to do that for him. And maybe he was worried, knowing how hard it is for artists to make a living..."

Chanelle hesitated. What was she doing? She had no business speculating on his personal situation or feelings toward his father. She was here to listen to what he had to say, not to give him a social worker's take on his relationship with his father.

A muscle flickered along Vance's jawline. His eyes had narrowed and he was looking at her intently, but Chanelle had a feeling he wasn't really seeing her at that moment. And then he turned abruptly and strode to a curving alabaster staircase that led to the second floor.

Passing the closed doors of the bedrooms where he said Mariah, Adrien and his mother were resting, Chanelle followed Vance through a long hallway to a central foyer with an antique drop-lid desk, built-in bookshelves and two recliners. When he gestured to Chanelle to sit down, she complied, her pulse quickening.

Okay, here it comes, she thought, trying not to look as cynical as she felt. *The excuse for kissing me like the ship was about to go down, then leaving me in the lurch to take up with a Zodiac employee.*

She bit her lip. Despite the rather personal exchange between them a few minutes ago, the fact remained that he had some explaining to do.

Why was he staring at her like that? He wasn't waiting for her to begin, was he? Because if that was the case, she had plenty she could say to him, starting with—

"Chanelle, before I get into what I really want to say, I have to thank you..."

Chanelle couldn't help making a sound that came out as a half laugh, half cough. "You're kidding me. For *what*, exactly? For providing you with some onboard entertainment?" She tossed her hair back and stared at him pointedly.

She was satisfied to see his eyebrows furrow and a hurt expression cross his features.

"Ouch," he said softly. "Chanelle, you've got it wrong. And I promised to explain—"

"I think I can figure it out," she said, raising her eyebrows. "As I might have mentioned before, your reputation precedes you. Leopards can't change their spots."

Vance clutched at his chest. "That's another arrow to the heart, Sagittarius. Didn't you see the sign on the tender? No archery allowed…"

"This is not a joking matter," Chanelle said curtly. She shook her head and stood up, heat sizzling through her veins. She strode to the French doors and stared out. The sun had disappeared, and the swiftly moving clouds were darkening. Just like her mood. She was already upset at *him*, but now she was upset with herself.

Vance sprang up from the recliner and strode over to stand beside her. "Look, Chanelle, please let me explain, okay?"

Chanelle turned to face him as a few drops of rain began to plop against the panes.

"I wanted to thank you for giving me your take on the situation with my father. My perspective has changed," he said huskily. "I gave up the playboy lifestyle after my father died."

His gaze shifted to the view. "I was too stubborn to promise my dad on his deathbed that I would carry on the business. And when he died, I was filled with guilt." He gazed back at Chanelle. "I realized I had to let go of some things. First of all, years' worth of resentment for a father who had spent more time at his job than with his kids. And second, life as a playboy." His eyes pierced into hers. "This leopard *has* changed, Chanelle. No spots in the last nine months. And the woman you saw me with is our director of environmental operations. She came by to drop off a gift for me since she wouldn't be at the gala."

Chanelle raised her eyebrows, remembering Vance's unbuttoned shirt and the hug he and the woman had shared.

"I was hugging her because she was leaving this morning to meet her fiancé in George Town," he said, as if he had just read Chanelle's thoughts. "They're getting married at the end of the week and then going on their honeymoon." He gave Chanelle a few moments to digest this information. "She's not only a great employee, but she's become a good friend. And in case you heard mention of a surprise in Toronto, I was referring to a surprise party from the staff to congratulate them on their wedding."

Chanelle pursed her lips. So if Vance had given up his playboy ways, why had he paid any attention to *her*? Kissed her so…so—

Vance stepped closer to Chanelle. Her pulse rate had increased exponentially as Vance had proceeded with his explanations and now, with him standing so close that she could feel his breath on her forehead, she was overwhelmed by a feeling of light-headedness. She looked up at his firm jawline and curves of his mouth, and when her gaze met his, the intense look in his blue eyes startled her. She inhaled sharply as Vance leaned down to kiss her.

She had wanted to ask him why he had left her stateroom so abruptly, what he had meant when he had said, "I'm sorry, but I don't want to stay and have you regret it later…" but his kiss blocked her words. And now his lips were moving over hers with a gentle pressure that was sending a swirl of desire throughout her. When he suddenly clasped her and deepened his kiss, Chanelle felt her thoughts and unspoken words scatter.

She wanted to believe him.

And she wanted this fantasy to continue...

Chanelle felt her sense of caution dissipating with the intoxicating pressure of his lips on hers. She wrapped her arms around his neck, and with the deliberateness and precision of a skilled Archer, she slid her fingers under his T-shirt to where the Aquarius waves were tattooed on his back. Pressing him closer, she returned his kiss with the passion that he had ignited, confident that her invisible arrow was hitting its mark.

Vance could feel his heart thumping erratically as Chanelle responded to his kiss, and when they finally broke apart, he realized the extra pounding was coming from the fat drops of rain pelting the French doors. A flash of lightning appeared, followed by a crackle of thunder that made Chanelle jump.

Sudden rain showers were common enough in these parts, and he was sure that this one wouldn't last long. He was disappointed, though. He had hoped to walk along the beach with Chanelle and show her around the island...

He wrapped his arm tighter around her. Her

face had paled and her green-hazel eyes were blinking. "My, what big eyes you have." He smiled at her. "Don't worry, Chanelle, the house won't blow down. It's a good thing we're here, though, and not out on the water."

"I'm not worried… I guess. But I think you're referencing two different fairy tales."

He laughed. "But there's a wolf in both, right?"

"Yes, and I'm hoping there are no wolves in sheep's clothing around here."

Vance couldn't resist leaning in to nibble Chanelle's neck, his pulse spiking when she gave a little shiver. "And what would you do if you came across one?" he teased.

"I'd distract him with custard-filled crois-sants," she shot back with a grin. "I'm sure he'd find them much more tasty…"

"I don't know about that," he murmured, leaning toward her again. Another clap of thunder reverberated around them, and Vance heard the alarmed voices of his mother and sister calling him from down the hall. His mother was probably worried that some windows were open and that the rain was pouring in. "I'd better check the windows," he said, squeezing Chanelle's hand.

"You're not leaving me here," she said. "I'm coming with you, Vance. I don't like big storms." She looked up at the ceiling as if she were afraid that it would cave in from all the rain. "Shouldn't we be hunkering down in the basement?"

Vance couldn't help chuckling. "You're in the Caribbean, Chanelle, not Canada. We don't have basements here."

They met his mother and Mariah in the hallway. Mariah rushed to him, grabbing his arm.

"I can't find Adrien," she cried. "I peeked in on him earlier and he was napping, so I had a snooze, too. When I heard the storm, I went to get him, and he wasn't there." She started shaking, and Vance took hold of her arms.

"Stay calm, Mariah. He must be in one of the rooms. You check the rest of the rooms on this floor, and we'll start on the main floor."

She ran down the hall toward the central foyer and where Vance's bedroom was located, calling Adrien's name. Vance turned to his mother. Her face was pale as well, and he felt his heart, which was already drumming over Adrien, twinge. "Mom, you and Chanelle wait downstairs. Chanelle, maybe put on some herbal tea for my mom, okay? I'll search for Adrien. He's probably doing a puzzle in the family room."

He gave them both an encouraging smile and descended the stairs two at a time. He hadn't wanted to show how worried he was, but as he filed through room after room with no sight of his nephew, a feeling of dread enveloped him.

By the time he returned to the kitchen, Chanelle was pouring the tea, and Mariah was running into the room. She burst into tears when she saw that Adrien wasn't with him.

"He—must be outside," she sobbed, trembling. "I'm going to go find him."

"No!" Vance said brusquely. "I'll go."

CHAPTER EIGHTEEN

CHANELLE POURED CHAMOMILE TEA into a cup as steadily as she could, not wanting to show how distressed she was. A child was in danger. Someone she knew, and someone who was precious to Mariah and her family. To the man she was losing her heart to.

"I'm going out to help Vance," she told them and rushed out of the kitchen as Vance's mother was formulating a protest.

Chanelle couldn't just sit there. She wasn't programmed that way. She had been trained to act with lightning speed when alerted to a dangerous or volatile situation involving a child. And right now, the storm was a danger. An enormous danger, with the intermittent lightning, slashing rain and what seemed like gale-force winds. She forced her mind not to think about any number of frightening possibilities as to where Adrien might be.

Chanelle was relieved to find another raincoat in the foyer armoire. It was oversized, but at least it would keep most of her protected. As she put it on, she decided that since Vance had gone out this way, he'd probably be checking the front of the villa and the covered boathouse. She would check the back.

As soon as Chanelle stepped outside, the wind whipped the hood of her raincoat back, and she knew it would be hopeless to even try to put it back in place. She wished she had at least put her hair up in a ponytail, which would have prevented her from being blinded at every turn by stinging strands of her hair along with the lashing rain. It was just early afternoon, but the sky had darkened ominously, and in the heavy downpour, Chanelle could barely discern what was two feet in front of her. An icy fear gripped her.

She prayed Adrien was safe...

Her sandals were soaked, and since the raincoat just came down to below her knees, her legs were drenched as well. It was hard to keep her eyes open, and she had to concentrate on which direction she was going. At one point she slipped into a flower bed that the deluge had reduced to a muddy soup, and she let out a cry at the stab of pain as her knees crashed into a decorative stone slab.

Her legs coated in mud, Chanelle regained her balance and continued toward the gazebo. She reached the pool area first, and her heart twisted at the thought that Adrien might have ventured into the pool.

But surely he wouldn't have dared without an adult with him…

With the reduced visibility, Chanelle had to skirt around the perimeter of the pool, peering in for any sign of Adrien. He had been wearing a red T-shirt…

Thank God, she murmured under her breath, seeing nothing. She plodded on toward the beach. She thought she heard a voice as the rain continued to pelt down, but the sound was quickly swallowed by the wind.

Chanelle was thoroughly soaked through. The raincoat had not been able to prevent the rain from streaming down her neck and drenching her dress right through to her bikini. She pushed her hair away from her eyes as a streak of lightning lit up the sky and made the area around her seem like something out of a supernatural movie. At the next boom of thunder, she made a dash for the gazebo, her heart responding with its own boom.

As she scanned the darkened interior, she spotted a hump in one corner of the gazebo. It looked red... She yelled out his name, and Adrien ran crying to her and wrapped his arms around her waist.

Vance ran as far as the boathouse, the blood pumping so hard in his veins that he was oblivious to everything but the sound of his own heartbeat. Who could have known that the weather would flip? And that Adrien would impulsively venture out of the villa?

He was five years old. And a boy who loved to explore around the island...

Vance backtracked and sprinted toward the shed near the rose garden. He glanced at the roses his mother had admired earlier, now flattened, with petals scattered all around the lawn.

Would Adrien have gone to seek shelter in the shed if he had been playing in the nearby sandbox when the storm had hit? Vance faltered at a sudden muscle cramp in his leg and came to a stop. He swore under his breath and bent to massage his calf, wincing at the pain.

When it eased, he continued toward the shed, walking as quickly as he could instead of running to avoid the risk of cramping up again.

Vance called out Adrien's name and looked inside the shed. Disappointment lumped in his throat. He prayed that Adrien might have made his way to the gazebo, the only other outside structure on that side of the property.

As Vance passed in front of the villa, the front door opened, and his mother called out.

Had she and Mariah found Adrien in some unsuspected place inside?

He stopped, chest heaving, only to hear his mother say worriedly that Chanelle had gone out to look for Adrien as well, and she had seen her heading toward the back of the villa.

The lump in Vance's throat slid and landed in his gut like a boulder.

In heaven's name, why hadn't Chanelle stayed put? Now he had two people to worry about. *Two people he loved.*

Cramp or no cramp, Vance sprinted around to the back, yelling out Chanelle's name. His hood had flown off long before, and he couldn't be bothered to keep it over his head. He clenched his jaw as thunder rumbled around him, and he prayed that Chanelle and Adrien were nowhere near areas vulnerable to lightning strikes.

He reached the pool and scanned the water that was agitated by thousands of needlelike raindrops. Now he knew what *desperate* felt like. With an ache in his heart that made him cry out, he made a run for the gazebo.

Vance knew that he had only been outside for minutes, but somehow it felt like an ordeal of hours. He reached for the canvas flap, and seconds later, he wanted to collapse in relief as his eyes made out the huddled figures of Chanelle and Adrien in the corner near the hammock.

Vance called out Chanelle's name at the same time that she called out to him. He ran to her and Adrien and hugged them tightly. "Thank God you're both safe," he said hoarsely, not having the heart to scold either one of them.

"I just got here," Chanelle told him, her voice trembling. "I couldn't just stay inside—"

"We'll talk later," Vance said brusquely. "Let's get out of here. Wait," he stopped her as lightning illuminated the canvas panels. "Okay, Adrien, come with me," he urged when the flashes stopped. "Chanelle, stay right beside us. We'll go in the sunroom door." He took off his raincoat and put it around Adrien before lifting him up and carrying him across the property and past the pool, looking over his shoulder at Chanelle every few paces.

Vance set Adrien down once they were in the sunroom. He called out to Mariah, and in moments, she was running toward them, crying in relief.

Adrien hadn't said anything up to this point, his face frozen in shock, but when he saw his mother, he ran into her arms. "Mommy, Mommy. I was so scared."

"I know, baby. Mommy was scared, too."

Vance's mother was close behind, and when she reached them, she hugged Adrien tightly, despite the fact that he was dripping wet, the raincoat dwarfing him. "Run a nice warm bath for him, Mariah, and I'll get him some milk and cookies after I grab some towels for these drenched souls."

Mariah turned to hug Vance and then Chanelle, despite their dripping state. "I can't thank you enough," she said tremulously.

"Chanelle found him in the gazebo," Vance said, keeping his voice steady.

"You're an angel." Mariah hugged her again.

"A true guardian angel." She stepped back and then looked down with a frown. "Chanelle, you're bleeding."

Vance turned to look. Below Chanelle's raincoat, her legs were smeared with mud and trickles of blood. "I'll take care of her, Mariah."

When they had gone, Vance helped Chanelle out of her raincoat. Her clothes were just as plastered as his, the only difference being that her knees and legs were bare and his weren't. He frowned upon closer inspection of her scraped knees. He wrapped a towel around Chanelle and brushed the last towel quickly over his hair and body before flinging it onto a wicker chair.

"You leave me no choice, Chanelle," he said firmly, "but to play doctor with you." And before Chanelle could respond, he lifted her up in his arms and made his way through the villa and up the alabaster stairway to his bedroom.

CHAPTER NINETEEN

As CHANELLE FELT herself being whisked up by Vance's strong arms, she had no choice but to clasp her arms around his neck, her heart thudding like a jackhammer. She closed her eyes as he proceeded up the stairway, anticipating a very uncomfortable landing should he lose his balance and fall...

But he didn't miss a step or even falter, as if carrying a woman up the stairs this way was something he was used to doing.

Chanelle opened her eyes and let out her breath. They passed the center foyer where they had been sitting earlier, and after a few moments, Vance paused at a set of double doors and reached for the handle. Chanelle caught her breath at the sight of the four-poster king-size bed and the stunning Lawren Harris painting above, a winter landscape that didn't seem at all out of place in this villa.

Vance's bedroom.

He carried her to a roomy walk-in closet revealing a row of shirts and pants and shelves with at least a dozen pairs of footwear below. "I hope you see something you like in here," he said, setting her down, and although she couldn't see his face just then, she could tell he was smiling. "Because you're going to have to get out of your wet clothes."

Chanelle's mind whirled. "Maybe Mariah has something I could borrow?" She looked down at her yellow dress, its thin cotton material plastered to her body and revealing the navy bikini underneath. Her neck started prickling with discomfort, and she pulled the towel more snugly around her.

"Maybe," he said, his gaze telling her that he had observed the revealing state of her clothes. "But she's busy now, and I'm not going anywhere until we fix up those knees. Before they get infected..."

He motioned for her to proceed into the ensuite bathroom and to sit down on a black leather chair near the marble-sided shower stall. Chanelle was dazzled by the gleaming luxury of the room, with its sleek granite countertop, floor of diagonal white and black marble tiles, and crystal spiral light fixture.

"I can take care of them," she told him. She winced. "I'll just need—"

"Don't move, Chanelle," he said firmly. "I have everything I need in my medicine cabinet. Now just hold tight and it will be over in a few minutes…" His mouth quirked. "You look like a wet little duckling in that yellow dress. And no, not the one in the fairy tale," he added quickly. "Quite the opposite."

She flushed. He was delusional if he thought she looked *pretty*. She had caught a glimpse of herself in the large vanity mirror above the black granite countertop. Her hair framed her face in tangled ropes, and her eye makeup had smeared and run under her eyes in black and navy streaks.

Yeah, real pretty.

Vance strode over to a gleaming white cabinet, withdrew a few items and deposited everything on the side table next to Chanelle. "I'll be back in a second," he told her.

She was tempted to start cleaning up her knees on her own. He had brought over a bottle of antiseptic, some sterile cotton gauze sponges, a couple of wide bandages and some antibacterial ointment. But as she went to grab the bottle, he returned with a chair from his bedroom.

He wagged a finger at her. "Now, now, Miss Robinson…" He deposited the chair opposite her, grabbed a lined wastepaper basket and set it down beside his chair. He washed his hands in the sink, and Chanelle felt like squirming when he glanced in the mirror a couple of times and caught her watching him. After drying his hands, he sat down on the chair.

"Okay, let's do this." He took a deep breath and poured some of the antiseptic on a gauze sponge. He leaned forward and was eye to eye with Chanelle. "I'll need your leg, miss," he murmured.

Chanelle stared at him. He raised his eyebrows. "Oh…" She blinked.

Did he want her to stretch out her leg on his lap?

He held out his hand. "May I?"

"Okay."

What else could she say?

She was already barefoot, having removed her soaked sandals in the sunroom. She extended her leg slowly and tried to keep her breathing steady as Vance put one hand under her calf and the other under her ankle before placing her right leg on his left thigh.

"Okay," he repeated. "Now this might just sting a lit—"

Chanelle let out a cry as the antiseptic soaked into the scraped areas, and her arms flailed, throwing the towel off her shoulders.

"I'm sorry, Chanelle. I know it must sting like hell. But we have to clean it out."

"Just hurry," she replied through gritted teeth and gripped the sides of the chair. Chanelle closed her eyes as he poured and dabbed, using a new gauze pad for each area. She felt like her knee was on fire, and it took all she had not to jerk her leg and accidentally kick him in the face.

"Okay, there, there. Your wound is clean. I'm just going to put some of this antibacterial ointment on the bandage and cover it lightly."

Despite the throbbing in her knee, Vance's soothing voice was helping her to relax a bit. But he still had her other knee to tend to...

He set her leg down gently and lifted her

other one onto his thigh. "Okay, here goes. We're almost done."

"You haven't even started the torture," she retorted, her eyes already closed.

"You're being very brave, Chanelle," he said solemnly before applying the antiseptic.

This time she did jerk her leg as she cried out, and when her foot made solid contact, she opened her eyes to see Vance holding his hands over his mouth and jaw.

"Oh, my God," she cried. "I'm so sorry. I didn't mean to kick you."

"I think some teeth are loose and are about to fall out," he said, his voice muffled behind his hands. "Oh, well, it's a good thing I've given up my status as a playboy." He shrugged. "Because I'm pretty sure being toothless is not one of the prerequisites."

Chanelle watched anxiously as he moved his hand away, expecting to see blood and teeth spill out. He gave her a sudden grin, and she saw that his teeth were intact.

Perfectly intact.

She glowered at him. "That was not necessary. You scared me."

"I'm sorry, Chanelle." He gave a soft laugh. "I just couldn't resist…"

She pursed her lips and then smiled. "Apology accepted. I'll *try* to resist kicking you again." She closed her eyes and then reopened them. "But I can't promise."

"Duly noted. Now let's finish this operation. My other patients are waiting."

Chanelle felt a warm stirring inside at their banter. And then clenched her teeth as Vance proceeded with the next round of dabbing. When the second bandage was in place, Vance looked at her quizzically.

"I've cleaned all around your knees," he said, "but we still have to get some mud off you." He looked pointedly at the streaks on her lower legs.

"I can do that myself," she told him. "I'll sit on the edge of the tub and wash it off." She eyed the streaks her feet and legs had left on his jeans. "And I think you'll need to wash up as well, Dr. Vancelot. And dry."

She felt a warm rush as he smiled at her, his eyes a startling azure. "Um… I'll just need a clean towel," she added.

"Right in the tall cabinet," he murmured.

"And I'll use the guest washroom in the room next door." He strode to the door. "You should change into dry clothes right away, Chanelle." His gaze dropped to her legs. "My pants certainly won't fit you, but I do have a pair of light pajamas with a tie belt." His mouth curved. "I'll leave them and some T-shirts on the bed for you...and Mariah can find something for you afterward."

Vance let the warm jets of water pulsate over his body in the guest room shower. He felt some of the tension ease out of his neck and shoulder muscles. For all his levity with Chanelle a few moments ago, he hadn't been as relaxed as she might have thought.

First of all, the fear of what might have happened to Adrien had made every nerve and muscle in his body so tight that he could still feel a residual ache. And then learning that Chanelle had gone out...

Discovering them in the gazebo had made Vance almost collapse with relief. But he had had to be strong for the both of them. Strong physically and emotionally. The physical side had been the easy part. Carrying Adrien inside and then carrying Chanelle upstairs, no sweat. It had been the emotional part that had drained him. Staying calm when he wanted to scream his frustration at every minute of his search that had proven fruitless.

In these past nine months at the helm of Zodiac Cruises, Vance had taken his position seriously, and as he had vowed after his father's death, he had stepped up to the plate and taken control. Out in the storm, he had felt all control slipping away from him. He had not been able to control either Adrien or Chanelle from going out and potentially putting themselves in danger.

He could have lost either one of them.

A lightning strike, a heavy falling tree branch, a misstep causing them to slip into the water or hit their head on something and pass out—any of these situations could have happened.

Vance had experienced the feeling of pure helplessness out in the storm.

And it had shaken him to the core.

But despite this feeling, his instinct to protect his family had kicked in. Every last neuron in his body had been primed to battle the elements and bring his loved ones back home safely.

Home. It wasn't the villa, beautiful though it might be. Home was the people in it, the people you loved.

His home was his family.

And Chanelle.

The storm had shaken up his thinking, too. His thoughts about commitment, about trust.

And if he had hesitated in the past about commitment, it was simply because the right woman hadn't been in his life at the time.

Chanelle was the right woman. He felt it in his gut. And he was ready to shift the scales in his life and find a balance between work and love.

Images of Chanelle flashed in his mind, from the first time he had seen her grab hold of Adrien with her white jeans and fuchsia T-shirt, to her elegant skirt and black top in the Mezza Luna Ristorante, and to that sexy white dress splashed with red poppies... And the yellow dress she was wearing now, wet and clinging to her body, revealing her bikini underneath...

Yes, her physical beauty had aroused his

senses, but it had been her inner beauty that had touched his soul. Chanelle was kind, sensitive, courageous, funny, hardworking...and she loved kids.

His pulse quickened at the thought of having children one day...a thought he had never seriously contemplated until now.

But that would mean having a woman—Chanelle—being as committed to him as he was to her.

Aren't you jumping the gun a bit? His inner voice shoved its way into his consciousness. *You haven't even told Chanelle that you want to be in a committed relationship. You just told her you've given up your playboy lifestyle, explained about Pauline, and then you kissed her. Get with the program, buddy. If you want her, you'll have to get more creative. A kiss alone isn't going to do it.*

Vance smiled ruefully. No, he *hadn't* made it clear to Chanelle how he felt. But the storm had made his feelings clearer to *him*. Now he just had to figure out how and when to communicate those feelings to Chanelle.

Vance stepped out of the shower and dried himself brusquely with a large, plush towel before changing into white Bermuda shorts and a turquoise shirt.

In the shower, Vance had come up with a crazy idea that would show Chanelle how committed he was to her…but he needed to sketch out his ideas on paper. And once he was satisfied with his plan, he would present it to her.

When Vance returned to his room, he was disappointed that Chanelle had already gone. He checked the time on his phone. They had about an hour and a half before the tender returned to pick them up to head back to the *Aquarius*. Looking out his balcony doors, he was relieved to see that the storm had diminished significantly to a light sprinkle, and the skies had brightened. There was no danger that they wouldn't be able to return to the ship.

He sat down at his desk. He would work on his idea before going downstairs. And if he didn't get the chance to share it with Chanelle before heading back, he'd save it until later tonight at the gala.

CHAPTER TWENTY

CHANELLE HAD FELT a little strange, sitting on the edge of Vance's bathtub in her bikini, rinsing off her legs. How could she *not* imagine him soaking in it, with the jets sending water swirling all over his body?

It was so unnerving...

He'd laid out three T-shirts and a pair of pajama bottoms with alternating loons and red maple leaves—that reminded her of the tie he'd worn for the Canada evening—and the words *Loony for You* on the rear.

Really? In any other situation, she would have found the Canadian-themed pajamas amusing, but all she could think about was how ridiculous she would look in them. With a sigh, she changed into a black T-shirt and the pajamas and headed downstairs.

At least her face and hair no longer looked like she had come out of some lagoon, she thought. Chanelle found Mariah and Adrien in the kitchen. Mariah laughed when she saw the loony pajamas. "Don't mind me," she said. "I can't help cracking up every time I see those. Can you tell Vance is a proud Canadian? Right down to his pajamas. And boxers. But don't tell him I told you." She laughed again.

"Don't tell me what?" Vance said, entering the room. "That Adrien's eating all my cookies?" He winked, ruffling Adrien's hair.

"Nice pants, Chanelle," Vance continued, chuckling. "You're welcome to keep them as a souvenir."

Chanelle's mouth dropped, and Mariah burst out laughing. "I can see how thrilled you are, Chanelle. Come on, let's go wash and dry your clothes and see what we can find for you in my room."

Chanelle was aware that Vance was watching them as they walked out of the room. Or more specifically, *her*. His gaze had swept over her T-shirt, and she had a feeling that his gaze was now taking in the *Loony for You* on the rear of the pajamas.

Upstairs, Mariah waited for Chanelle to get her wet dress and bikini and then proceeded to the laundry room. "They shouldn't take long," Mariah told her. "I'll put them through the quick cycle."

"There's no point in me borrowing your clothes, then."

"Okay, well, do you want to come back downstairs or wait in the guest room? There's a fabulous window seat with a great view, and a pile of books and magazines."

"I can wait in the guest room, thanks."

"No, thank *you*, Chanelle. Please know that you're welcome to visit us here any time."

The guest room was bright and roomy, with coastal decor. The linens were done in white and sky blue, with big accent pillows in a fresh butter yellow. Chanelle sat down at the window seat and looked out at the brightening sky, trying to figure out why she felt a sudden sense of foreboding.

Soon they would be back on the ship, and Coral Haven would be just a memory. She just wished she had been able to explore the island a little more, walk on the beach, swim in those jeweled waters…

It had been kind of Mariah to invite her to come back and visit, but what reason would she have to come back to the Kingstons' private island?

Soon the cruise would be over, and she would have to make a decision about her job. That was the reality she faced. And sharing passionate kisses with Vance Kingston wasn't going to change that reality. How could it?

The anxiety she had felt searching for Adrien made her realize that she had also been anxious about returning to the same job. Important though it was, it was also highly stressful, and she had had more of her share of stress these past years.

You're stronger than you think, Vance had told her. *You'll know when the time is right.*

Maybe it was time to look at a career change.

No, there was no maybe about it. It *was* time. Time to find something in a related field that wouldn't take all her energy. That would allow her to lead a more balanced life.

There! She had come to a decision! As soon as she returned home, she would start her search for a new job. And a new life. Chanelle automatically reached for her bracelet and realized with a jolt that it wasn't on her left wrist.

And then she remembered…she had left it on one corner of the tub.

She would run in and retrieve it before Vance came back upstairs. And then she'd grab her clothes, dry them, get dressed, return to the ship and enjoy her remaining time on the cruise before getting back to reality.

A reality that didn't include Vance Kingston.

While she was exploring other job options in Sault Ste. Marie, Vance would continue his job as president of Zodiac Cruises in Toronto. He had said that his playboy lifestyle was finished, and maybe it was.

But the way he kissed you…

So Vance had gotten carried away after some emotional sharing about his father…and so had *she*. But that didn't mean Vance wanted anything more. She had been a temporary diversion. He had encouraged her to have fun on the cruise. Live a little.

She would be crazy to think that Vance Kingston could figure in her life after the cruise.

Chanelle bent forward to pick up her bracelet, trying to ignore the sudden heaviness in her chest.

"Nobody ever showed me they were 'loony for me' quite like that before."

Chanelle froze outwardly, but inside, it felt like a lava flow.

She straightened and turned around, holding out her bracelet. "I came back for this," she said as evenly as she could. The room seemed to be closing in on her. She couldn't breathe. She needed air.

She wanted out. Out of the room, out of the villa, and off the island.

And away from Vance.

Away from the man she knew would only ever be a fantasy…

Chanelle was too hot in Vance's black T-shirt. It was making her suffocate. She wished she could just tear it off. And the stupid pajamas, too. She needed to go and get her clothes.

Now, before she…

Vance leaped to catch Chanelle as she fainted. Her face had been flushed, and he had thought it was embarrassment at his comment—which he had instantly regretted—but he suspected that it was something else. Perhaps something to do with the barometric pressure, since she *was* highly sensitive to changes in temperature.

Vance's heart began to pound.

Was she breathing?

Her body had flopped onto his chest, and her head was drooping to one side. He placed his cheek against Chanelle's neck and felt the fluttering of her pulse. Relieved, he lifted her and carried her to his bed, where he set her down gently.

Vance raised both her feet and stuck a pillow underneath, while watching her mouth and eyes for any sign of movement. Had she been too hot? He couldn't very well remove her shirt, though. He put her feet back down and felt for Chanelle's pulse on the side of her neck.

Thank God, or he would have had to initiate CPR…

Vance leaped to the minibar fridge for a bottle of water. She'd need it when she regained consciousness. He set it down on his night table before leaning forward to feel for her pulse again. Watching her filled him with a sudden feeling of tenderness that made the backs of his eyes sting.

And a feeling of terror.

She needed to come to. Calling for emergency services would take far too long.

"Come on, Chanelle, my love. Wake up. *Please.*" He brushed a kiss on her forehead.

She gave a soft moan, and her eyes fluttered. And opened.

Vance let out a deep breath. *Thank God.*

Chanelle tried to move.

"No, Chanelle. You have to stay still for at least fifteen to twenty minutes."

"Why?" Her eyes widened. "Where am I?"

"Shh. You're on my bed and you've just regained consciousness."

"From what?" Her eyes widened. "We didn't…"

"No, silly. From fainting. And you scared the hell out of me," he said gruffly. "For the second time today."

Her brow wrinkled. "Why?"

"Why are you asking so many questions?" He felt her forehead. "Just relax. You might be dehydrated. Here, have some water."

He put the bottle to her lips while supporting the back of her head with his other hand. She lay back down, and her hazel-green eyes pierced his. "Why?"

"You're a stubborn one, aren't you? Okay, do you really want to know why, Chanelle? It's because I... I—"

"Vance?" Mariah called from the hallway. "The tender is here."

CHAPTER TWENTY-ONE

CHANELLE WATCHED THE island recede until she could no longer make out the coral walls of the villa. In reality she had only been there for hours, but it had seemed so much longer… and now she was leaving with this inexplicable feeling that she had lost something before she had had enough time to figure out what it was.

When Mariah had called out to Vance, his mouth had clamped shut, and whatever he had been about to say was left unsaid. He had left quickly, and a moment later, Mariah had entered his room to keep an eye on Chanelle. Chanelle had closed her eyes, not feeling up to chatting. After ten more minutes of lying still, she had risen slowly to find that Mariah had retrieved her dry clothes. "Come down when you've changed, Chanelle. The tender is waiting for us."

As they all left the villa moments later, Vance tried to catch her eye, but Chanelle deliberately avoided his gaze. He offered a hand as she was about to step into the tender, but she ignored it with the pretense of helping Adrien. Vance frowned and looked sideways at her, but she continued moving on.

Now, heading back to the *Aquarius*, Chanelle focused on the shifting blues of the sea.

Better than focusing on the shifting blues of Vance's eyes, she thought cynically.

It was choppier going back, a residual effect from the storm. By the time they boarded the ship, Chanelle's stomach was feeling unsettled. She couldn't wait to go back to the privacy of her stateroom. She'd order a soothing pot of herbal tea and maybe a bite to eat later, if she was up to it. As they waited in the lobby for the elevator, she said as much to Mariah, who quickly reminded her about the gala later in the evening and the champagne art auction. "Have your tea, Chanelle, and a rest, too, but please come to the gala. It's the highlight of this cruise! We'll save you a place at our table, okay?"

Chanelle felt a heat searing her nerve endings, knowing that all eyes were on her. Especially Vance's. It was even worse once they filed into the elevator. His breath fanned her neck, and the spicy cedar notes of his cologne tickled her nostrils. When the bell sounded and a couple excused themselves to exit, there was more shifting, and Chanelle felt Vance's hands encircling her waist to gently indicate that they needed to get by. Chanelle started and took a step sideways while her heart did a somersault.

She held her breath as the door closed, expecting Vance to move his hands away, but as the seconds ticked by in her mind, they stayed put. Chanelle felt sure everyone could see her flaming face, and she was just as sure that Vance could feel her erratic breathing reaching the span of his hands.

Another group needed to exit, and this time, Vance complied with Chanelle's silent wish. Hers was the next stop, she thought, breathing out her anxiety. At the ding, she stepped out and turned to wave. "Thanks again." She smiled, focusing her gaze on Mariah and Vance's mother. "Have a good evening." She turned away quickly, letting out a big sigh of relief as she heard the elevator doors close.

Chanelle repositioned her beach bag over her

shoulder and started to walk toward her stateroom when she heard footsteps behind her.

"Chanelle..."

Chanelle turned slowly and stared into cobalt depths that made her feel that she had just entered the eye of a storm.

"You're looking at me like I'm a boogeyman, Chanelle." Vance ventured a crooked smile.

"I—I just wasn't expecting you to follow me," she said without smiling back.

Vance was puzzled. Was she upset at him about something? It was obvious that the dynamic between them had changed. Maybe her fainting spell had something to do with it.

"You looked like you wanted to be alone in the tender, so I didn't want to bother you, Chanelle. I figured you had a headache." He took a couple of steps closer to her. "How are you feeling now?"

Vance saw confusion flitting across her face.

"I'm fine," she said curtly.

"Well, I'm glad I was there to catch you before you hit that marble floor," he told her huskily.

"Yes," she said, her voice softening slightly.

"I don't think I thanked you for that." She nodded. "Thank you."

"You're very welcome, Chanelle." He paused as the elevator opened and let out a family. When they had filed down the corridor, he closed the gap between himself and Chanelle. "I'll walk you to your stateroom."

Vance was convinced there was something bothering her.

Why else would she be treating him so indifferently?

Her kiss before the storm hit had been anything but indifferent... It made his stomach flip just thinking about it.

What had changed? Certainly not *his* feelings. If anything, they had intensified when he saw her lying on his bed and thought of how devastated he would have been if he hadn't been there and she had fallen to the floor and seriously hurt herself.

Vance realized with a jolt that Chanelle had stopped walking and was at her door, looking at him pointedly, her hand on the doorknob.

"Chanelle, I wanted to talk to you back at the villa before we left..." He looked at her earnestly. "There's something I need to say to you." He watched as her eyebrows furrowed. His gaze lowered to her lips and to that tiny turquoise vein pulsing at the base of her neck. Vance felt his jaw tensing. He wished he could just kiss her now and leave no doubt in her mind as to how much he wanted her…

"I'm sorry, Vance," Chanelle said stiffly, turning the door handle. "I think it's best if you go."

CHAPTER TWENTY-TWO

OUR LIVES ARE galaxies apart and always will be.

Chanelle hadn't had the nerve to tell him that to his face. But since she had woken up from her fainting spell, it was as if the fairy-tale fog she'd been in had lifted from her mind and now she could see the situation for what it was. She had thought about nothing else during the ride back to the *Aquarius*.

Chanelle closed the door firmly and plopped herself down hard on the couch, wincing as the muscles stretched in her knees.

Nice shape you're in, girl. Your knees are scratched up and now your heart is broken.

It served her right. How ridiculous to have fallen for Vance Kingston in the short time she had been on the cruise. What had she expected? That the president of Zodiac Cruises would be captivated by her brooding disposition and declare his undying love and affection for her?

Yes, they had shared a passionate kiss, a kiss that had had her yearning for more. Vance had swept her off her feet—both figuratively, sending her into wispy clouds of fantasy, and literally, carrying her up a grand flight of stairs like in some old-fashioned movies she had enjoyed watching before life had gotten too busy with her work.

But she had to listen to the voice of reason in the back of her mind. The niggling voice that was telling her that this physical attraction between her and Vance wasn't going to end up like a fairy tale. How could it? In a few short days, she'd be stepping off the ship and making her way back home. The idea that Vance Kingston was contemplating anything more than a casual flirtation with her was simply ridiculous. *A fantasy.*

And *she* had to make it clear to him that she wasn't going to encourage any further contact with him. Because although she had every intention of staying rooted in reality, she knew that there was always a chance that being alone with him could weaken her resolve...just like the spicy cedar scent of his cologne weakened her knees and made her want to—

She was obviously more vulnerable than she had thought.

Chanelle let the tears well up, feeling sorry for herself and even more sorry that she couldn't cry on anybody's shoulder. When her tears were spent, she walked out to the balcony to watch the sky and the sea as twilight began to set in. Since she wasn't hungry and had no intention of attending the gala, she would take this time to explore some options about her future.

Chanelle placed a hand over her bracelet. Becoming a social worker hadn't been a bad choice. Working in child protection had just become too much for her. Maybe a highly sensitive person like herself would have a difficult time thriving in such a stressful, emotionally charged job for her entire career…and maybe the five years she had devoted to this area of social work was all she was meant to do. But what other job *could* she do?

Chanelle looked up at the sky, a palette of blue, pink and magenta. Something deep inside told her that she would discover the answer if she kept open to new possibilities.

Send it out to the universe!

How often had she read *that* advice in self-help books?

"Okay, I'm sending it out to you, universe!" she called out to the sky before going back inside.

She couldn't let this thing with Vance destroy her peace of mind. She was stronger than that. She had to accept the fact that they had been physically attracted to each other and that was all. And if she wanted to be open to new possibilities, she needed to get herself out of her stateroom and allow herself to live a little.

Maybe she'd go to the gala after all.

What would there be to lose? She could handle it. She'd enjoy the musical entertainment and the complimentary champagne at the art auction, and then she'd sleep in tomorrow and enjoy one last sea day before they arrived back in Tampa the morning after.

And then she'd be ready to start a new chapter in her life.

Do you really think you can handle going to the gala? You're taking a risk—

Chanelle squeezed her eyes shut, as if the action could put a stop to her HSP voice. It had worked for her in the past, allowing her to be cautious, be safe. Protecting her from frightening possibilities...

Her eyes flew open. What was there to be frightened of? Yes, she was taking a risk. But that wasn't going to stop her. She was a Sagittarian, wasn't she?

They had chosen to have the gala on the top deck. A section of the Constellation Club had been cleared for the ship musicians, and after the official announcements, they would be performing a medley of popular tunes from the last four decades.

Vance clapped along with the guests after his mother thanked them for joining the staff of the *Aquarius* in celebrating her retirement. Her tribute to Vance's father had moved the audience.

After the applause subsided, she called Vance up to join her. She looked at him for a moment, her mouth quivering slightly. "I can only imagine how difficult it has been, son, for you to have accepted the challenge of taking over

264 CARIBBEAN ESCAPE WITH THE TYCOON

where your father left off…" She bit her lip, and Vance felt a lump form in his throat.

This was difficult for her, too. It had always been difficult for her, raising him and Mariah single-handedly most of the time. He hadn't been the only one who had suffered…and now he could see that she had also suffered for him, lacking a proper relationship with his father.

"I'm so very proud of your commitment, dedication and hard work, Vance. You've proven yourself—as I knew you would—not only to your family, but to the entire company, and there is no doubt in my mind that your father would have been just as proud." Her voice trembled at her last phrase, and Vance felt his eyes begin to mist along with hers.

"So, with all my love and pride, I congratulate you for your leadership, and I'm absolutely thrilled to officially name you president of Zodiac Cruises."

Vance blinked a couple of times to keep his emotions in check as he and his mother embraced. When his vision cleared, he looked beyond the clapping hands to his sister's table. Mariah was there with Adrien, but she was not looking in his direction. She was waving at someone. He followed her gaze and spotted Chanelle standing near a column.

She stepped forward, and what he saw took his breath away. She was wearing a floor-length deep purple satin gown with a filmy silver shawl over her shoulders. And she had arranged her hair in a side-swept style, held back with something that glittered under the string lights. His pulse hammered against his veins as he watched her walk over to sit next to Mariah. She waved to Adrien and said something to make him laugh.

Vance heard his name again, and he turned and saw that his mother was looking at him with raised eyebrows.

It was his turn to speak.

He hadn't written out a speech; he knew exactly what he had to say. After thanking his mother for trusting him to carry on the business, he announced his new plan: a new cruise line that would cater to social service organizations, offering their employees a special discount for a Zodiac R&R Cruise. Not only would the employees get the rest and relaxation that they so greatly deserved, Zodiac would treat them with special perks and discounts in all areas of the ship. The first ship in the fleet would be in operation by the following year.

"Society doesn't always recognize the tremendous work and sacrifices made by social workers, nurses and teachers, to name a few," he said, scanning the crowd. "Zodiac Cruises wants to support those who support others." He paused as the guests applauded enthusiastically and, glancing in Chanelle's direction, saw that her attention was riveted on him.

Great—if he could figure out a way of speaking to her alone, he could tell her the rest of his plan...

Vance thanked everyone for choosing Zodiac Cruises and for sharing in the celebration. He guided his mother toward their table, relieved that the entertainers would now be in the spotlight before the art auction began.

He had some unfinished business with the beautiful lady in purple...

As they approached the table, he saw a man stooping to talk to Chanelle, and a moment later, he was leading her toward the other dancing couples.

Where had this guy come from?

Vance tried not to make it obvious that he

was watching them as he helped himself from the hors d'oeuvres tray that one of the waiters was holding out to him.

Vance had no idea what he had just swallowed. His thoughts had returned to Chanelle's abrupt manner after her fainting spell.

As he had changed into a white shirt and black suit, he had wondered why Chanelle's behavior toward him had shifted from sizzling hot to disturbingly indifferent. Could she be deliberately repressing feelings for him that went deeper than the physical chemistry that they had both felt? She was probably holding back, believing that they would never see each other again after the cruise.

He would find out tonight, he had vowed, adjusting his tie. And if Chanelle decided not to attend the gala, he would find a way to see her and clear things up with her. Make her understand that he wanted *her* in his life after the cruise. And forever. With that resolution, Vance had made his way to his mother and Mariah's stateroom, feeling much lighter than before.

It wasn't going to be easy to approach Chanelle now, though, with a man having suddenly appeared out of nowhere to whisk her away to dance. They seemed to be chatting easily, and Vance felt a stab of jealousy. *He* should be the one holding Chanelle. He rose, intending to cut in for the next dance, but a few guests stopped to congratulate him and his mother, and he had no choice but to engage with them for a few minutes.

When they moved on, Vance strode toward a less crowded section of the deck, where the smooth operator had managed to lead Chanelle.

Luck was on his side this time, he thought smugly as the song came to an end. But the fellow did not let go of Chanelle.

And had his hand slipped down to her hip?

"May I have this next dance, Chanelle?" Vance gazed at her first, but before she could answer, he turned to stare pointedly at the guy, his mouth curved slightly but his eyes sending a clear "Back off" message.

The guy released his hold on Chanelle, smiled awkwardly and told Chanelle he'd see her in a bit.

Like hell you will, buddy.

Vance nodded with a congenial smile and took Chanelle's hand.

His other hand settled around her waist. He felt her stiffen, and when his gaze met hers, her eyes seemed to be shooting sparks at him from their hazel-green depths.

And then she pressed closer and went on tip-toe to place her cheek against his. His pulse leaped as her lips brushed his cheek and ear-lobe.

"I *don't* want to dance with you," she hissed in his ear.

CHAPTER TWENTY-THREE

CHANELLE FELT VANCE'S body tense up. She hadn't meant to sound so rude, but the words had escaped before she could think of another way to give him the message.

"Why not, Chanelle?" he said, with genuine curiosity in his voice.

Chanelle was taken aback. She didn't know what she had expected him to say, but she certainly hadn't expected him to ask her to explain. Now she had to answer. And there was no point mincing words. She turned to meet his gaze. "I—I don't want to dance with someone who…who makes me want more…when I can't have more." Chanelle felt her neck prickle with heat at the intensity in his eyes. They had some kind of magnetic pull that kept her from looking away. And to make it worse, the musicians started performing "Stairway to Heaven." The string lights suddenly dimmed, and Vance drew her closer.

"What makes you think you can't have more, Chanelle?" he murmured against her ear as he initiated the slow dance. "You've got your facts wrong."

Chanelle's heart was jumping hurdles. "But the cruise will be ending in two days..." She felt his lips brush against her earlobe and rest there as they danced. The touch made her nerve endings sizzle and her body shiver at the same time.

"Chanelle, let me say what I wanted to tell you at Coral Haven. You're an enchantress—who looks absolutely stunning in purple, I must say—and someone whom I'd like to continue to see even after the cruise ends."

Chanelle froze and as Vance's words sank in, her feet and arms feeling woozy. The couples dancing around her became blurred, and the music seemed to pulsate right through her body. And then she felt Vance's arms tighten around her, and her arms rose of their own accord and wrapped themselves around his neck. Her cheek grazed his chin, and when their eyes met, it felt like nobody was on deck except them and the music was playing for them alone.

Vance's gaze was intoxicating, and when he

pulled her tightly against him, she marveled at how her body fit right into his. They slow danced for what seemed like forever, and when the song finally came to an end, Vance nuzzled her earlobe again and whispered, "Chanelle, do you believe me?"

She opened her eyes with a start, and as some of the couples dispersed, she saw Mariah walking up to them. She broke away awkwardly from Vance.

"Hey, you two," she smiled. "We're heading back to our stateroom. Adrien's starting to nod off. But don't stop dancing on our account. Good night, Chanelle. Good night, *Sir Vancelot*. Don't drink too much champagne…"

As they left, there was an announcement that the art auction would begin after the next mix of songs, and the champagne would start to flow. At the beginning of a classic rock song that everyone started singing to, Vance lifted an eyebrow. "Stay or go?"

"Go," she told him. "I want to end the evening on a quiet note."

"It's quiet in my stateroom."

Chanelle felt a moment of panic. She was at a total loss as to what to do next. Here she was, having just danced as close as two people could possibly get, and she couldn't seem to process Vance's words that she was someone he'd like to see after the cruise, let alone his invitation to go to his room.

He had asked her if she believed him. *Maybe...a little...*

There was no doubt in her mind that there was chemistry between them.

Incredible chemistry.

But he hadn't said *I'm in love with you* or *I want to spend the rest of my life with you.* He had just said she was someone *he'd like to continue to see...*

And there was no guarantee that came with the Vance Kingston package, the guarantee that he wouldn't leave her in the future. Just like her father and Parker had done...

Chanelle's mind filled with doubts.

Maybe they had both been swept away by their physical attraction to each other...and that was the extent of it.

"Chanelle, you're frowning. Are you okay?"

"I—I'm just tired," she said.

She was tired of exhausting herself by trying to analyze Vance's every word or action.

She knew that this was part of her highly sensitive nature, and sometimes—many times—she wished she could just sail along in life without her brain getting twisted up in knots about everything.

What was wrong with her? She was sure most women would jump at the invitation to join Vance in his stateroom.

"Chanelle, if you're too tired, can you just come to my room for a few minutes? There's something I've been designing for Zodiac Cruises, and I'd love to get your input." Vance's eyebrows lifted as she waited for his response.

Chanelle searched his eyes and saw nothing but earnestness in them.

But what if—?

No! She wasn't going to let her doubts control her this time. She was just going to allow herself to sail along for once. Vance's words popped back in her mind: *You're stronger than you think.*

Yes, she was strong enough to handle anything the future had in store for her. But it had taken a little help from Vance to remind her of her inner strength. Her sense of self. She needn't be fearful of anyone abandoning her anymore, least of all herself. She was a Sagittarian, wasn't she? Vance had called her that enough times to make her come to the realization that she had power over her life, her choices, her loves...

And no one could ever take that away from her.

"Sure," she said decisively. "I can spare a few minutes."

Vance led Chanelle toward the sliding doors leading to the elevator lobby. The gala was in full swing. The captain and some of his crew were drawing a lot of attention, so Vance knew his absence wouldn't be obvious. The guests were drinking, dancing and having fun, and they would be happy about another photo opportunity with a handsome man in uniform. Or three. The art auction would begin shortly, then more music, followed by an unexpected surprise: a spectacular display of fireworks. Mariah and his mother would be watching from their balcony, and maybe Adrien would be, too, if he was still awake.

As he and Chanelle approached his stateroom, Vance felt his stomach contract with anticipation. He had thought long and hard about how to tell Chanelle about his feelings. About how he couldn't imagine her stepping off the ship and never seeing her again. About how he couldn't stop thinking about her, and how she had inspired him...

And now, he finally had the opportunity to show her. As he swiped his card against the door plate, he glanced at Chanelle. She was holding her clutch purse and looking down, biting her lip. Was she having second thoughts? His heart hammered softly. She was the kindest, most sensitive woman he had ever met. And the only one who had managed to break through the defenses around his heart. The heart that was finally ready to let someone in.

With any luck, he'd convince her tonight that they belonged together. *For life.*

CHAPTER TWENTY-FOUR

CHANELLE SAT DOWN on the edge of the couch and watched as Vance strode over to his desk. She wondered if what he was designing had something to do with his plans for Zodiac's new cruise line. His announcement that the latter would cater to social service organizations, offering their employees a special discount for a Zodiac R&R Cruise, had jolted her.

In a good way. How could she fault him or his company for being sensitive to people like her?

And when Vance had added that Zodiac Cruises wanted to support those who supported others, Chanelle had felt a stirring in her chest, pretty sure that he had been looking right at her. And then moments later a gentleman had appeared and asked her to dance...

Chanelle hadn't really been in the mood, but her nagging inner voice had reminded her about her intention of enjoying herself tonight.

She sat back on the couch now and tapped

her fingers on the cream-colored leather hand rest. The sky's earlier brilliance had faded to dusky blues and pinks, with fading ribbons of gold and magenta. She tried to stifle a yawn.

"Hey, don't fall asleep yet," Vance chuckled, sitting beside her. "First I'd like your two cents about my design."

"Sorry, it's been a day."

"You *are* tired." He gazed at her for a moment and added softly, "This won't take long."

Chanelle looked at the sketch pad in his hands. "Does this design have something to do with your new cruise line?"

Vance's eyes crinkled as he smiled. "It sure does."

"That's a great idea to offer special packages to service organizations." She had to give him that.

"Thanks. I've been working on the idea of a new line for months now," he murmured. "But I was stuck on the purpose behind the line. I wanted to find a new angle, and I did…because of *you*, Chanelle."

Her eyes widened, and her heart started a gentle drumming. "Wh—what do you mean?"

"You made me see what can happen to a dedicated employee in your line of work. How important your job is, and how you give your all to help others. People like you need to be rewarded, not get to the point where they burn out. But sometimes burnout happens, to social workers, teachers, nurses, etcetera." He tapped her gently on the arm. "So *that* became my angle. Supporting those who support others."

Chanelle watched Vance open up his sketchbook and prop it up so she could see what he had done. She gave a soft gasp at the first drawing. *Of her.* Her thoughts swirled, and she couldn't bring herself to look up from the page. As he turned the next few pages slowly, the drumming in her heart became magnified. She saw a series of rough sketches with variations on the new name for the R&R cruise line. And then he turned to the last page with a finished sketch.

Chanelle's heart stopped.

She saw two intertwined Cs in the words *Chanelle Cruises*, with each C extended to represent waves in the sea and an archer's arrow zooming upward. She stared at it for a few moments, and when she looked up, Vance's face was blurred. She wiped her eyes and saw that his eyes had misted also. And then Chanelle remembered what she had thought earlier, that Vance hadn't told her he was in love with her or that he wanted to spend the rest of his life with her. No, he hadn't told her.

But he had just shown her.

Chanelle gazed at him in wonder.

Was she dreaming? She must be dreaming…

Vance closed the sketchbook and placed it on the coffee table. She felt immobilized as he reached over to grab something leaning against his side of the couch. He turned it toward her and she gasped. It was the painting she had admired in the art gallery. *Enchantment.*

She was speechless as Vance stood up and propped it against the back of the couch.

"Is that…" Her gaze dropped to the initials, and her eyes widened. "Did *you*—"

"Yes, it's one of mine." He gave her a sheepish smile. "The art rep mentioned that a guest was admiring it. And she noticed your name on your lanyard." His blue eyes gleamed. "It was going to be in the art auction, but I replaced it with another painting when we returned on the ship. I wanted you to have this one."

She gasped as he suddenly dropped to one knee.

"I have fallen under the spell of your enchantment, my lady," he said huskily, taking her hand and kissing it. "Will you do me the great honor of bestowing me with your hand?"

"You already have it, Sir Vancelot," she murmured with a soft laugh.

"I was speaking of your hand in marriage, my haloed beauty." He grinned, caressing her hair with his other hand. "In anticipation—and hope—of your positive response, I have begun to design your engagement ring...but in the meantime, I hope this humble handmade gift will suffice."

Several loud pops filled the air. "Come with me, Chanelle," he said urgently. He led her to the balcony, and as they stood at the railing, they heard a whizzing sound and more popping as the sky sparkled with the most dazzling fireworks display Chanelle had ever seen.

They watched for a few minutes and then Vance turned her toward him and, wrapping his arms tightly around her, kissed her thoroughly, sending sparks to every last inch of her body. When he released her, his eyes pierced hers, reflecting the flashes in the sky.

"Do you believe me, Chanelle?" he said huskily, repeating the question she hadn't answered earlier. "And will you—"

"I do," she breathed, and reached up to show him with her own kiss.

Vance gave a moan of pleasure. "I almost forgot to add," he said, while brushing soft kisses along her neck, "Zodiac Cruises will be in need of a director of children's activities. Someone who loves kids and can plan year-round events that are fun and safe." He paused to gaze deeply into her eyes. "I must warn you, though. Job hours vary and may require some night shifts…and plenty of cruising."

Chanelle felt a sudden flutter in her gut. Was she actually ready to leave her small-town world and take such a leap? To a new city, new job and, most important of all, a new relationship? Her gaze melded with his. What she saw in the depths of Vance's ocean-blue eyes was a bright promise…

Yes, she was quite ready to take that leap.

"I'll cruise with you anywhere and every-

where," she sighed, slipping her hand underneath his shirt to caress his back. She felt him
shiver as her fingers brushed over his Aquarius tattoo.

"I love you, my Sagittarian angel," he murmured against her ear as the boom in the sky
intensified. Without waiting for her to answer,
he scooped her up in his arms and carried her
to his bed, where Chanelle knew the fireworks
were only just beginning...

* * * * *

LET'S TALK
Romance

For exclusive extracts, competitions
and special offers, find us online:

- **f** facebook.com/millsandboon
- **⊙** @millsandboonuk
- **𝕐** @millsandboon

Or get in touch on 0844 844 1351*

For all the latest titles coming soon,
visit millsandboon.co.uk/nextmonth

Want even more
ROMANCE?

Join our bookclub today!

'Mills & Boon books, the perfect way to escape for an hour or so.'

Miss W. Dyer

'Excellent service, promptly delivered and very good subscription choices.'

Miss A. Pearson

'You get fantastic special offers and the chance to get books before they hit the shops'

Mrs V. Hall

Visit millsandbook.co.uk/Bookclub and save on brand new books.

MILLS & BOON